I DARE YOU!
A Moments in Maplesville Novella

Farrah Rochon

Nicoba

Special thanks to my critique group members, Shauna Roberts, Rosalind Green Holmes, Margaret Hauck and Laurie Bolanos, for helping to come up with the perfect dares for this book.

And to Phyllis Bourne for always being a great sounding board.

I DARE YOU!

A Moments in Maplesville Novella

Chapter One

Bullshit! You're gonna chicken out!

Stefanie Sutherland-Thomas's fingers flew across the touchscreen as she pounded out a reply to her best friend Tania's text message.

I won't! I'm doing it. And with someone hot!

She pressed send then locked her cellphone before slipping it into the pocket of her too-form-fitting-for-her-own-comfort capri pants. She adjusted her back against the unforgiving bamboo barstool she'd occupied for the past twenty minutes, and tried once again to recall just what it meant to relax. She remembered the concept, but damn if she could figure out how to actually do it.

Wiping a trail of condensation from the hurricane-lamp-shaped glass, Stef took a deep pull on the straw that poked through the pineapple, orange, and maraschino cherry garnishing the tropical drink.

Her phone vibrated.

"Really, Tania?" She tugged the phone from her pocket again and laughed at the latest message.

I want proof, Tania had texted. *If you don't send proof, I'll know you chickened out.*

Stef shook her head as she typed.

How am I supposed to send you proof? Just trust me. You dared me. You know I never back away from a dare. Now stop texting. I'm on vacation.

She put the phone away — for good this time — and took another sip of the icy punch.

Her shoulders wilted with contentment. "Oh, that's good."

Stef tilted her head back and peered up at the beach bar's thatched roof, its dry reeds rustling from the strong breeze that blew in from the west. She tapped her fingers to the melodious rhythms of a steel-drum band that carried on the wind, providing the perfect soundtrack to the start of her short vacation. Her very much needed vacation.

"How is it going here?" came a lilting island voice. She twirled her stool around and smiled at the handsome bartender. "Would you like to try a rum punch this time?" he asked.

"No, thank you," Stef said. "I don't drink alcohol."

She raised the glass to her lips and peered at him above its rim. His rich mahogany skin stood in stark contrast to the peach and cornflower-blue print shirt the staff at the resort wore. He was a little on the young side, but she wouldn't hold that against him, not in this particular instance. A cute, young hottie with nicely muscled arms and a pretty smile would work just fine when it came to taking on Tania's dare.

And she *would* take on this dare.

Her best friend had been taunting Stef for months, accusing her of becoming a boring homebody who was too afraid to step out of her comfort zone. Tania had only made things worse when she sent Stef a bunch of selfies from her spur-of-the-moment cross-country motorcycle trip on the famous Route 66. It was just the kind of thing Stef once loved too. These days, trips to the post office were scheduled in her day planner.

Crazy and spontaneous were no longer a part of her vocabulary. They couldn't be. She had a seven-year-old son to raise and a demanding job that didn't mesh with the untamed, impulsive person she used to be. She'd silenced that Stefanie a long time ago.

But she'd never meant to cling so fiercely to the other end of the spectrum.

She'd been so determined to become the docile, well-behaved daughter her father could be proud of. A disciplined soldier, an agreeable wife, a nurturing mother. She'd done such a good job that she could hardly conjure a mental image of the girl she had been all those years ago. And that's when she'd accepted that her friend was right—she was a boring homebody, a shadow of her former self. The realization had both shocked and repulsed her.

That's why, when Tania had challenged her to do something wild and spontaneous while on vacation and away from the responsibilities she'd left back home, Stef had accepted the dare. There was nothing wrong with being a little uninhibited. That's what escaping was all about. What happened in the islands stayed there, right?

And what would be crazier than having a one-night stand with a random stranger?

You know you won't do it! Tania's voice rang in her head.

Actually, that sounded more like *her* voice.

It *was* her voice, because Stef's sensible side knew darn well that if she went through with this, it would be a mistake she would live to regret. However, the other side—the side that was ready to get laid after a drought that had lasted way too long—nudged the wicked little devil on her shoulder into action.

Wild and spontaneous.

She could drum up that girl she used to be just for tonight, couldn't she?

"Bartender?"

"Yes?" He walked over to her, slinging a towel over his shoulder. "Can I get you another fruit punch?"

"Not yet, but thanks," Stef said, adding a tinge of sauciness to her voice. If she was going to do this, then she'd better do it. She was only here for two and a half days.

Before her common sense could talk her out of it, she said, "There is...ah...something else you can give me, maybe when you get off work?"

And then she winked.

The look of instant horror that flashed across the bartender's face sent every bit of bravado Stef had built up plummeting into the crystal-blue waters that surrounded the island.

Had she really just said that?

She suddenly had an overwhelming urge to jump down from the barstool and race back to her room. Hell, back to the airport. If it wasn't for her twin brother Stefan's wedding tomorrow, she would call her few hours in Turks and Caicos a wrap and haul ass back to Louisiana.

"I am so sorry," Stefanie said. "I don't know what made me say that."

What was she doing? Other than making a fool of herself, that is.

The bartender's tentative smile held several shades of discomfort. "I get it a lot. It comes with the job."

Goodness, had his voice sounded so young before? He was a child!

"I truly am sorry," Stef said again. "That was extremely inappropriate."

"Really, it's okay, ma'am."

Ma'am? Great. He'd probably lumped her in with the desperate cougars that hit on him every day. If humiliation were a prize at the state fair, someone would be pinning a blue ribbon on her chest right about now.

11

With another smile—this one slightly less uncomfortable, but still awkward—the bartender went back to diligently wiping down the surface of the already pristine countertop. She was pretty sure it was relief that flashed across his face when a patron on the other side of the semi-circular bar summoned him.

Stef's eyes fell shut while mortified tremors continued to quake through her belly.

Well, she could scratch the hot bartender off the list of eligible men with whom she could have a little naked island fun. It was pretty pathetic that, so far, he had been the *only* man on her list.

Fearing that a repeat of any eye contact would have her melting into a puddle of embarrassment, Stef twirled her stool around to face the beach. As her gaze scanned the white sand that stretched for miles, she lost confidence that she would find *anyone* to take the spot the bartender had vacated on her one-night-stand candidate list.

It was obvious her brother, Stefan, and his soon-to-be wife, Callie, had chosen a resort that catered to couples to host their destination wedding. It made sense. Of the handful of close friends and family that had been invited to join them on Grand Turk, Stef was pretty sure she was the only one who was unattached.

"Good looking out for the single gal," she said with an indelicate snort.

Although, she wasn't all that surprised that Stefan and Callie hadn't taken into account her relationship status as plans were being made. When her friends and family looked at her, they didn't see *single Stefanie*—they saw *widowed Stefanie*.

Which apparently meant she shouldn't feel like a ninth wheel around the other couples who would be here this weekend.

But she did. She felt like a lonely, desperate, undersexed ninth wheel that scared off cute bartenders with her sharp cougar claws.

Maybe she *should* add some rum to her fruit punch.

Nah, she and alcohol had engaged in a short, brutal relationship. The one time she'd tried it she'd become so sick that she'd never touched the stuff again. Besides, if by some miracle she *were* able to find someone to help her take on Tania's dare, she wanted to be sober enough to enjoy it.

But there had to be a better way for her to occupy her time. She wasn't sure how much longer she could endure sitting here under the hot July sun, sipping fruit punch like her life depended on it and making a fool of herself with her dismal attempts at flirting.

The rest of the wedding party and guests, who had all arrived yesterday, were sailing around the crystal-clear waters surrounding Grand Turk on a catamaran, no doubt having a great time as they enjoyed early evening cocktails. Stef had been delayed a day, flying first to Tampa to escort her seven-year-old, Jacob, to his grandparents, her late husband Brandon's folks. Stefan had offered to remain behind so that he could be here when she arrived at the resort, but Stef wouldn't hear of it.

Now, she was sorry she hadn't taken her twin up on his offer. Watching all these loving couples walking hand in hand on the beach was giving her heartburn. She had no problem admitting that she was jealous as hell. It had been a long time since a man had taken her by the hand and looked at her with longing in his eyes.

Another pair of gooey-eyed lovers came up to the bar, taking the two stools to her left. She was forced to stomach a full five minutes of their giggles, playful kisses, and soft caresses.

Just as she was about to toss her drink on them to cool them off, Stef heard, "Is this seat taken?"

She looked to her right and stopped just short of having a coronary. Standing before her was the personification of tall, dark and gorgeous.

"No, it's not," she answered.

He gestured to the stool. "Do you mind?"

"Not at all."

Yes, honey, why don't you sit your cute butt right on down.

14

In less than five seconds, Stef had determined three things that made Mr. Tall, Dark and Gorgeous a prime candidate to help her accomplish her dare. No wedding ring, just enough wrinkles bracketing his mouth to indicate that he was over thirty, and no twittering twenty-something on his arm.

Oh, yeah, he was definitely going on the list. He wasn't just on the list—he *was* the list.

As he climbed onto the barstool, her new neighbor smiled one of the most stunning smiles Stef had ever seen. Oh, wait. She *had* seen that smile before. She saw it every time she got sucked into a *Criminal Minds* marathon and saw Shemar Moore's devastating dimples twinkling back at her. His skin was nearly the same golden brown as the bamboo stool he'd slid onto, and his face had just enough beard scruff to make her insides tingle at the thought of how it would feel rubbing against…interesting places.

Stef crossed her legs and bit back a moan. Goodness, but she was horny.

Mr. Gorgeous tapped on the bar to get the bartender's attention, then turned her way and gestured to her drink.

"Can I buy you another?"

"Sure," Stef said, even though she'd already consumed more fruit punch today than she had all of last year.

He motioned to the bartender who—damn him—definitely looked relieved that Stef had found someone else to flirt with. She made a mental note not to come back to this particular bar for the rest of the trip. The resort had at least a half-dozen others to choose from.

"A Turk's Head Stout for me and a second of whatever the lady is having," her new neighbor ordered.

"Thanks," Stef said.

"My pleasure." That dimple peeked out again. "One of the perks of visiting an island resort like this is the opportunity to buy a beautiful lady a drink, isn't it?"

A crack of laughter shot from Stef's mouth before she could rein it in. "Wow. You're not even going to ease into this, are you? Pulling out the heavy artillery before I even know your name."

She was rewarded with a flash of brilliant white teeth as he held his hand out to her. "I'm Dustin, and I'm not really known for my subtlety."

"That's quite alright. Subtlety is overrated," she returned. "I'm Stefanie."

"Pretty name for an equally pretty lady. What brings you to Grand Turk, Stefanie? Vacation?"

She nodded. "And you?"

"The same," he said.

The bartender returned with their drinks. Dustin tipped his dark beer bottle toward her glass. "Is that a drink, or a fruit salad?"

Stef laughed again. "A combination of both."

"You have a beautiful laugh," he said.

Oh, he wasn't even trying to be sly with his.

As if he'd read her mind, his grin broadened and he said, "When it comes to a beautiful lady I'm looking to impress, I'm shameless in my flirting."

"I can tell." Awareness cascaded down Stef's spine. "It just so happens that you've come across a woman who has no problem at all with a handsome man calling her beautiful. Lucky you."

He turned his barstool so that he was fully facing her. "I have to ask, Stefanie, why is such a beautiful woman like yourself sitting at this bar alone?"

She nearly let it slip that her vacationing companions were out touring the islands, but then remembered that despite the gorgeous dimples and the fact that he was currently the sole occupant on her dare-eligibility list, he was a complete stranger. She did have a bit of self-preservation floating somewhere in her head.

"I wanted to enjoy the view, but my friends can't take the heat so they're at the bar inside," Stef answered. "What about the people you're vacationing with? Or do you enjoy coming to couples' resorts alone?"

"No, no, no." He took another pull on his beer before continuing. "I'm here with a few friends. They're out island hopping, but, unfortunately, work followed me from the States and I had to sit in on a conference call."

Setting her elbow on the bar, Stef cradled her chin in her palm and, with amusement tinting her voice, said, "It sounds as if you need a refresher course in what it means to be on vacation. The point is to leave work at home, not bring it with you."

"Touché."

An adorably chagrinned smile emerged, playing at the corners of his mouth and sending those addictive tingles skipping along her skin once more.

"I was upset that I was missing out on all the fun," he continued as he leaned back, tracing a finger around the lip of his beer bottle. His warm gaze dropped to her mouth, and a ribbon of heat instantly curled through Stef's blood. "I'm not anymore. There's nothing they're seeing on that tour that can capture my attention as much as what I've found right here at this bar."

Oh, he was as smooth as butter melting over a hot biscuit. And just as scrumptious. Stef couldn't deny that she was falling for his charm hook, line and sinker.

And that was just fine with her.

She hadn't flirted with a handsome man since well before her deployment to the Middle East. She couldn't really call what she did back then flirting anyway. She'd lost her husband in a car accident the year before, and had just started to entertain the idea of dating again when her unit was called to action two Thanksgivings ago.

Her stunningly gorgeous bar mate had caught her at a vulnerable period in her life, and a part of her was grateful for it. If ever there was an ideal time for her to throw caution to the wind and engage in the casual island hook-up Tania had dared, it was now.

Their conversation progressed from shameless flirting — on both their parts — to more substantive discussions, like which was tastier: conch fritters or corn fritters. And who was the best Bond: Pierce Bronson or Sean Connery. Or, her favorite debate, which was better: red Kool-Aid or purple. The man actually picked purple. Even worse, he called it *grape*. He was clearly insane.

Stef's eyes widened in surprise when she glanced over her shoulder and discovered that dusk had fallen.

"Something wrong?" Dustin asked.

"Not really. I just didn't realize how much time had passed."

"Do you have somewhere else you need to be?"

The trace of disappointed panic she heard in his voice massaged her still-tender ego. After the way the bartender had fled, it was flattering to have a man who actually wanted her attention.

"No," Stef answered. A slow, seductive

smile eased across her lips as she recalled his earlier assertion. "Besides, I doubt there's anything on this island as fascinating as what I've found here."

The naked heat that flashed in his eyes scorched her nerve endings. She was playing with fire; that much was obvious. They'd spent these past few hours engaging in increasingly sexual word play. Flirtatious. Sensual. Addictive.

Stef had found herself on the brink of inviting him to her room more than once. She wanted her one-night stand, and she wanted it *now*.

But she was enjoying his company so much that she didn't want this to end too soon.

"So," Dustin said. His fingers inched towards her, tentatively at first, then more boldly, his thumb caressing the gentle bend of her wrist. "I now know that you have horrible taste in James Bond actors. It makes me wonder what else I can learn about you."

"Such as?"

"Oh, I don't know. Like what do you do when you're not beautifying the beaches of Turks and Caicos with your presence?"

Stef couldn't help the sharp laugh that escaped her lips.

His brow scrunched in a slight grimace. "Was that too over-the-top?"

She held her fingers up and pinched them

close together. "Just a bit. But don't let that stop you. I'm finding you utterly entertaining."

"At least I'm good for something." He smiled. Those dimples were killing her. "So, what do you do, Stefanie? If you don't mind me asking."

"Not at all." She drained the last of her watery fruit punch before continuing. "I spent ten years in the army, four active duty and six in the Reserves. However, I'm back to living the civilian life. I'm an ER nurse at a small hospital in southern Louisiana."

Stef thought she saw concern in his eyes, but his expression cleared so quickly she wasn't sure if she was mistaken.

"What kind of business are you in?" she asked. "It must be something high-pressure if it pulled you away from hanging out with your friends on the islands."

"I'm in the oil and gas industry," he answered. He waved it off. "Boring stuff. I doubt you want to hear about it."

"Oh, I don't know about that." Stef set both elbows on the bar and rested her chin on her folded hands. She'd decided a while ago that he more than fit the bill for her dare, but getting to know him a little better wouldn't hurt.

She smiled up at him. "Try me."

Dustin's gut twisted in horrified disbelief as realization dawned on him.

This was Stefan's sister. His damn sister!

From the moment he'd first encountered her sitting at the bar he knew there was something familiar about her, but he couldn't quite put his finger on it. Something with the way her mouth edged up when she smiled, the way her eyes tilted slightly at the corners. After she mentioned being an army nurse, her resemblance to her twin brother hit Dustin square in the chest.

Stefan Sutherland was his best friend. He'd spent the past three hours nursing a hard-on for his best friend's *twin* sister—his *widowed* twin sister, for crying out loud.

Concern for her was why Stefan had first moved to Louisiana in the first place. He was about as overprotective of his sister and her son Jacob as an ex-military guy could be. Stefan would lose his shit if he found out Dustin had spent the evening using some of the same pick-up lines on her that they'd perfected back when they both were navy men.

He had to find a way to pry himself out of this situation. Sisters were off-limits. It didn't matter that Dustin didn't have a sister; if he did, she would be on the prohibited list.

It also didn't matter that Stefanie had been flirting with him just as aggressively as he'd flirted with her. Or that on more than one occasion tonight she'd given him that look that said she would have no problem with him eating her for breakfast tomorrow morning.

Dammit. Now that image would be in his head for the rest of the night.

He needed to get out of here. Now. He couldn't do this to Stefan. Not only because he was his best friend, but because he was also the best flight instructor on Hawk Offshore Transportation's payroll, the helicopter shuttle company Dustin had started after leaving the navy six years ago. He was already dealing with his share of uncertainty where Hawk Transpo was concerned; he didn't need to heap on more by messing things up with Stefan.

Yet, despite all the reasons prodding him to bid Stefanie a goodnight, Dustin could not force himself to leave. Sitting there in that pink sleeveless top that showcased her nicely-shaped shoulders and well-toned arms, she was exactly what he'd been looking for when he'd left his room. A fun, sexy, interesting woman who could help him forget about all the things clouding his mind. He needed this distraction too much, and it had been too damn long since he'd connected with a woman this quickly, for him to give her up anytime soon.

Her lighthearted teasing wrenched a laugh from him despite his efforts to dial back his interest. There was no use; he was interested. He would just have to deal with the consequences.

"How long are you in Turks and Caicos?" he

asked, even though he knew she would probably head back to the States with the rest of the wedding guests, save for Stefan and Callie, who were moving to a resort in Providenciales for their honeymoon.

"Monday," she said. "Most of my friends are leaving Sunday, but I'm giving myself an extra day to enjoy the islands."

Dustin was booked on the same Sunday afternoon flight back to New Orleans. Changing it to Monday wouldn't be all that difficult.

Whoa, there. He was getting a little ahead of himself.

A *little*?

Okay, a lot. He was ninety-nine percent certain Stefanie was going to be pissed when he showed up tomorrow at Stefan's wedding. He debated for a second whether he should come clean, but then tossed out the idea. He was too afraid she would walk away from him if she knew just who he was.

"So, do you have plans for Sunday, or are you planning to just be lazy?" Dustin asked.

"I'm not sure yet," she said. "How about you?"

He flashed the most charming smile in his arsenal. "Sweetheart, whatever plans I have can change the minute you give me a reason to change them."

The color that blossomed on her cheeks only urged him to think of other ways to make her blush. There were *so* many things he could do.

She sized him up with a suspicious look, her brows arching over warm brown eyes. "You claim you work in oil and gas, but I'm not buying it. I think you're a professional flirt."

"Nah." Dustin shook his head. "The flirting is just a part-time gig." He winked. "And only when I've found someone who's really worth the effort."

There was the blush again.

"So, what are your plans for the rest of the evening? Are you up for a late dinner?" he asked.

Her gaze roamed his face before settling on his lips. She shook her head, and in a husky whisper, said, "I want to do something wild and crazy."

Heat developed underneath his skin, a slow burn that steadily increased with every second that passed.

"Like what?" he asked.

Several moments edged by as she fiddled with the napkin underneath her glass. Finally, she said, "Earlier today a good friend accused me of being boring." For the first time tonight her expression became intensely serious. "I didn't like hearing that. She dared me to do something out of character, and she knows I've never been able to back away from a dare."

"What's the dare?"

"If I tell you, would you do it?"

25

"Depends on what it is."

Her gaze drifted back to his lips. "I think you would like it."

He swallowed. Swallowed again.

"Tell me," he managed to speak past the lust wedged in his throat.

She leaned toward him, her breasts brushing against his arm. "Take me to your room and I'll show you."

Her seductive murmur sent a shot of desire straight to his groin.

He hopped off the barstool so fast he nearly tripped over his own feet, but you couldn't pay him to care that he looked like an idiot. The only thing his mind could focus on was the sultry words Stefanie had whispered in his ear.

Dustin threw a fifty on the bar and grabbed her by the waist, hauling her down from the stool. His skin was hot. His body tightened with need as he watched her trek through the white sand beach. His eyes trailed from her trim ankles, to her shapely calves and firm, perfect ass. Her silky smooth dark-brown ponytail brushed against the small of her back. His hands clenched in anticipation as his mind instantly conjured an image of that luscious hair clutched in his fist, him tugging her head back as he took her from behind.

She's your best friend's sister! That's who you're thinking about taking from behind!

He couldn't think about the implications it

would have on his friendship with Stefan when he learned that Dustin had carnal knowledge of his twin sister. It didn't matter. Nothing would stop him from following Stefanie's incredibly hot body to his room and availing himself of everything she was offering.

By the time they arrived at the door to his oceanfront suite, Dustin felt ready to burst out of his skin. When he'd left this suite after his conference call earlier today, he'd embraced a distant hope that he'd find someone willing to engage in a casual hook-up. An hour or two of nice, hassle-free, stress-relieving sex — something to take the edge off all the pressure he'd been shouldering these last few months.

But he'd found so much more.

Dustin was willing to concede that there was nothing hassle-free about sleeping with his best friend's sister. Things were bound to get complicated, but he'd deal with that later. And he could forget one or two hours; he planned to spend all night learning every inch of that petite, well-toned body.

He opened the door and moved to the side so that Stefanie could enter ahead of him. She let out a low whistle when he turned on the lights, bathing the spacious suite in a mellow glow.

"These are some serious digs," she said. "You treat yourself well, don't you?"

"It's vacation," he said, tossing the room keycard on the table next to the door. "I thought

I'd splurge."

His fingers itched with the need to touch her, but Dustin held back. He didn't want to pounce on her like a horny teenager, even though a fifteen-year-old first-timer probably had more control than he could command right now.

Still, he had at least a small bit of the gentleman his parents had raised left in him.

"Can I get you a drink?" he asked.

Stefanie turned to him, her luminous, warm brown eyes filled with heat. "I had enough to drink at the bar." She pressed her fingers to the center of his chest. "I came here for something else."

Dustin went instantly hard as she backed him up against the wall.

Despite the primal need bursting through his bloodstream, he forced himself to ask, "You sure about this, Stefanie? This isn't just the alcohol talking, is it?"

That sexy smile drifted across her lips again. "Dustin, I haven't had alcohol in years. I was drinking fruit punch. Now, kiss me."

She flattened her front against his and thrust her tongue in his mouth.

Oh, hell yeah.

His arms went around her, his palms instinctively finding her ass. Damn, but it was a nice ass. Tight, firm, compact, and squeezable. He tugged her even closer as his tongue skated along hers. The low, erotic sounds rising from her throat drizzled down his spine like hot, sensual rain.

While one hand remained on that amazing ass, he inched his other hand up and under the hem of her snug tee, his fingers burning with need at the first touch of her bare skin.

Dustin brushed his thumb back and forth along the small of her back as he continued to explore her mouth. He closed his eyes and envisioned kissing her as he peeled the clothes from her body and laid her down in the king-size bed just down the hallway. He wanted to do that so badly his body ached with it.

Her hands roamed all over him, moving along his arms and up his torso. When her fingers brushed the bulging fly of his khaki shorts, he nearly lost it then and there. He needed to get her naked. Now.

"Stefanie. Clothes." He thrusts his tongue inside her mouth again before pulling back enough to speak a coherent sentence. "It's time to lose the clothes."

She nodded and pushed his shirt up.

Then she stopped.

Just like that, she stopped.

"Oh my God," she breathed through deep pants. "What am I doing?"

No. No, no, no.

The sensual haze that had smoldered in her gaze just a second ago was gone. Clarity had returned.

"I can't do this," she said. "Oh my goodness, I can*not* do this."

"It's okay," he murmured despite the protests shrieking in every cell of his body.

She took several steps back, her brilliant eyes bright with distress. "I'm so sorry," she said. "I swear I didn't mean to lead you on."

"It's okay, Stefanie," he said. "Really, it's fine."

"No, it isn't," she said. "You're so sweet and so much fun, and I really, *really* wanted to do this, but I just can't. I'm so sorry, Dustin, but I have to go."

Dustin expelled a deep breath and nodded. He reached for the keycard. "Let me walk you to your room."

"No." She stayed him with a hand to his arm. "That would be..." She let out a shaky breath as she tugged her shirt back into place. "That would be too much temptation."

"I'm not all that convinced that a bit more temptation would be such a bad thing."

She released a breathless laugh. "Yes, it would," she said. Her eyes softened. "Thank you so much for this afternoon. I had a wonderful time with you."

"I can say the same," Dustin said.

She reached for the door, but before turning the handle, looked back and said, "Please don't take this the wrong way, but I really hope I never see you again."

Then she turned and rushed out of his suite, closing the door softly behind her.

Dustin just stood there for several minutes, motionless, trying to rein in the scattered emotions rioting through him. He'd gotten *way* more than he'd bargained for when he'd embarked on finding himself a casual hook-up for the night. He should be alarmed at just how intensely he wanted her; instead the hair on the back of his neck stood at attention for an entirely different reason.

He wondered just how Stefanie would react tomorrow when he dashed her hopes as he stood as the best man at her brother's wedding.

Chapter Two

Stefanie bypassed the traditional boiled fish and grits that was purported to be a breakfast favorite among the locals. Instead, she opted for the array of fresh fruits displayed on the buffet table of the private veranda where Stefan and Callie's wedding day breakfast was being held.

Armed with a steaming cup of strong coffee and a couple of spears of fresh pineapple, Stef moved over to the far edge of the veranda, the breeze lifting the ruffled hem of her flouncy, ankle length sundress as she walked. The spot afforded a panoramic view of both the small gathering of family and friends that had managed to make it out of their rooms for the wedding day breakfast, along with the beautiful beaches beyond.

The sun was preening in the sky above the Atlantic's blue waters, its rays glinting off the gently cresting waves. Several resort guests had already taken to the private beach, their colorful beach towels contrasting against the white sand.

Stef didn't see any time for fun in the sand on today's agenda. This Saturday was all about watching her twin marry the woman of his dreams.

Stefan and Callie had originally planned to

get married back in November, but in early September Lieutenant Colonel Morris Sutherland's heart had almost given out. It had been a shock to everyone who knew him, because at sixty-one her father was the epitome of fitness. When her mother first called to tell her about it, Stef's initial thought was that his heart was a total badass to even think of disrespecting the Lieutenant Colonel in such a way. No one crossed him, even his organs.

Stefan had been just fine with their father missing the wedding, but Callie wouldn't hear of it. She insisted they postpone until the Lieutenant Colonel recovered from his heart attack. Her future sister-in-law had these grand plans of repairing Stefan's relationship with their father. Stef tried to tell her she was on a fool's mission. She was pretty sure those two began butting heads the second Stefan was born.

Stef looked around the veranda for the older man's gleaming bald head. She didn't see it. She wasn't surprised. She loved her father, but he was a stubborn bastard. She was sure he hadn't shown up at the breakfast just to piss off Stefan.

That was just fine with Stef. She was in no hurry to face the Lieutenant Colonel's oppressive scrutiny. She and Jacob had visited her mother and father over Easter, and months later Stef was still suffering the effects of those judgmental grunts and glowers of displeasure. She had made her way onto his list of massive disappointments years ago and had yet to make if off.

Stef spotted Stefan over by the head table. He looked happier than he had in years. It was fitting, seeing as today was the day he would marry a woman who was perfect for him.

Last night, however, he'd looked the opposite of happy.

When Stef had arrived at her room just past ten p.m., Stefan was waiting for her, half-crazed with worry. She'd noticed the six missed calls and dozen text messages he'd left on her phone as she was taking her pseudo walk of shame from Dustin's room last night, but hadn't bothered to return them.

When Stefan asked why she hadn't answered his calls, she'd lied, telling him that she'd forgotten to turn the phone back on once the plane landed. If he hadn't been so worked up he probably would have realized that she was lying since she'd texted him as soon as her plane had touched down yesterday afternoon.

She hadn't answered any of Stefan's attempts to contact her because she hadn't wanted anything to bring her back to reality. She'd had this one small snapshot of the old Stefanie, a brief glimpse of the girl who used to thrive on excitement. The girl who wouldn't bat an eye at doing something as spontaneous as picking up a guy at a bar, going back to his room, and showing him the time of his life.

Stef's eyes fell shut.

She was no longer that girl. She *couldn't* be her, even for a little while.

But she would be forever grateful to Dustin... *Dustin*... Goodness, she didn't even know his last name!

It was probably for the best. He was meant to be nothing more than a fleeting memory, a short-lived respite from her humdrum existence. When she was feeling overwhelmed with the mundane routine of her day-to-day life, she would remember the gorgeous stranger she'd met in the islands who, for a few hours, gave her a treasured peek at the old daring Stef.

Willing herself to put last night out of her mind, she looked out over the crowd. Callie and her two best friends, Jada Dangerfield and Kiera Coleman, were on the opposite end of the veranda, intensely studying one of the resort workers who was trying to show them a dance move they were probably learning for the reception after this evening's wedding. She looked toward the entrance and noticed her mother and father coming up the walkway.

Great. Better to get this over with. She'd been a nurse long enough to know that quickly ripping off a Band-Aid was better than slowly peeling it off the wound.

Stef set her breakfast on the wide railing and walked over to them. "Mom. Dad," she greeted.

Her mother greeted her with arms

outstretched, encompassing Stef in a hug and kissing both her cheeks. She stepped back and motioned to Stef's sundress.

"You look amazing as always," her mother said. "It's too bad Callie didn't choose light blue as her wedding colors. You could wear this to the wedding this evening."

"The sage green bridesmaid dress Callie picked out is even more beautiful," Stef said. She turned to her father.

"How is Jacob?" he asked.

Hello to you, too, Lieutenant Colonel.

"He's fine," Stef answered. "I talked to him this morning. Robert and Shelia are taking him to Disney World today."

"Oh, I know he's going to love that," her mother said.

Her father just nodded.

Stef inwardly sighed. It hadn't always been this way between them. At one time in her life, she'd actually communicated with the stoic soldier standing in front of her. Things had changed twelve years ago, when he'd had to step in and save her ass from the biggest mistake she'd ever made. More than a decade later and Stef was still residing on his bad side. Although, she wasn't certain he even had a good side anymore.

Her mother announced that she was famished and tugged the Lieutenant Colonel toward the buffet, effectively ending the awkward standoff.

Thank goodness that was over.

Now, if only she could get through the rest of the day without having to interact with him.

Stef turned and her heart stopped.

For a second she thought her mind was playing tricks on her. Dustin had just walked into the space that had been cordoned off for the private wedding breakfast.

She raced toward him, looking over her shoulder, trying her best to shield him from the rest of the wedding party.

"Good morning," he greeted with that sexy smile that she'd mentally stored away for those days when she needed a little pick-me-up. Warmth flooded her belly at the sound of his honeyed voice, and for the barest moment Stef cursed herself for not staying in his room last night and finishing what they'd started. How amazing would it have been to hear him waking her up with that rich, velvety voice?

Focus!

"What are you doing here?" she hissed. "You can't be here."

"Why not? This is considered a common area for resort guests."

"Not this morning. This is a private event. You can't be here," Stef repeated. She glanced over her shoulder again and lowered her voice. "I told you last night that I didn't want to see you again. Are you stalking me?"

She heard footsteps behind her and turned to find Stefan approaching, a huge smile stretching across his face.

Shit.

But then, in a move that had Stef questioning whether the bright Caribbean sun had blinded her, her brother bypassed her and went straight to Dustin.

"What's up, Hawk?" Stefan said, holding a hand out to the stranger she'd kissed up against a bedroom wall last night and bringing him in for a one-arm hug. "I was wondering if you'd make it to breakfast. You get everything taken care of on that conference call yesterday?"

What the hell?

"As far as I'm concerned," Dustin answered with a nod. "But knowing those guys at O&G Tech, they'll have a new set of demands by the end of the week."

Stef looked back and forth between the two of them, confusion billowing within her chest.

She turned to her brother. "Do the two of you know each other?" But before Stefan could answer, another thought occurred to her. "Wait a minute. You called him Hawk." She turned to Dustin. "I thought your name was Dustin?"

"It is," Dustin said.

"So why is my brother calling you Hawk? And why in the hell do you even know him?" *And, oh my God, please don't let this be what I think it is.*

But Stef already knew it was *exactly* what she thought it was.

She turned back to Stefan, and in a voice that was begging him to tell her she was mistaken, she asked, "Your boss's name is Hawk, isn't it?"

"Technically, my boss's name is Dustin Patrick. We just call him Hawk after the E2-C Hawkeye carrier he flew in the navy," Stefan explained. "Dustin, meet my twin sister, Stefanie."

"That is the dumbest nickname I've ever heard," Stef said, ignoring her brother's introduction. She'd had her tongue down this man's throat last night—introductions were unnecessary.

Stefan's brow wrinkled with his sudden frown. "What's going on here?" He looked from Dustin to Stefanie. "Oh, shit. Hawk, what did you do?"

The silence divulged as much as a full confession would.

Stefan groaned like a dying animal. "Really, man? My sister?"

"We didn't do anything," Dustin said, holding his hands up.

"Hey!" Stef smacked his chest. "What we did last night was *not* nothing. Do you think I go up to random guys' rooms all the time?"

"My *sister*!" Stefan said again.

"Oh, get over it," Stef said. She turned back to Dustin. "You knew who I was last night, didn't you? I cannot believe you didn't tell me that you're my brother's best man."

The edge of his mouth hitched up in the most deliciously wicked way.

"You never asked," he answered, his voice tinged with amusement. That same smile that she'd thought was so sexy a minute ago made her blood boil with rage.

And, yes, a bit of excitement too. Dammit.

Stef was so mad she wanted to hit him. "I cannot believe you."

"Why does it matter?" he asked.

"Why does it matter? You don't think me sleeping with my brother's boss matters—"

"Hold on," Stefan said, cutting her off. "I'm gonna need the two of you to stop talking. Right now. I'm not spending my wedding day imagining whatever did or didn't happen between you two." He pointed a threatening finger at Dustin. "Be glad I don't want to mess up Callie's wedding pictures with you standing there beside me with a black eye, because I'm ready to kick your ass."

"Nothing happened," Dustin said.

"Stop saying that!" Stefanie said.

"Just please stop talking. Both of you." Stefan tugged Dustin by his shirt sleeve. "Come on. Callie booked us appointments at the on-site barber to get all shaved and cleaned up for the wedding."

Dustin hesitated for a moment, his searing

gaze penetrating the wall of righteous indignation Stef had started to build around herself. She turned away, refusing to look in his direction.

With the express purpose of avoiding him, Stef returned to her room, staying there until it was time to join Callie, Kiera and Jada in the suite where they were getting their hair and makeup done before the wedding.

She joined the wedding party on the beach at the start of the sunset ceremony, but when Dustin tried to speak to her, she sailed past him, not giving him a chance to say a word before he had to move forward in his role as best man.

As she stood on the white beach, watching Stefan and Callie exchange their vows, Stef was blown away by how beautiful her sister-in-law looked in her gorgeous bone-colored sheath wedding gown. It flawlessly curved over Callie's willowy frame; its elegant, sweetheart neckline adding the perfect touch. The simple bouquet of deep purple orchids completed the picture. There was no doubt about it, Callie was breathtaking.

Stef tried her hardest not to cry, but seeing the love radiating between her brother and his bride was too much for her sentimental heart to withstand. She could not be happier with the woman Stefan had chosen to share his life with. She already felt as if Callie was the sister she had always wanted.

As difficult as it was, Stef staunchly avoided Dustin's gaze. But every time she happened to catch it, he was looking at her, his eyes piercing her with entreaty. She ignored him. She wasn't ready to forgive him just yet.

Once the wedding was finished and the post-ceremony party began, dodging him looked as if it were going to be next to impossible. There were only fifteen people in attendance, Stefan and Callie's closest friends and family, so the chances of avoiding any one person was practically nil, especially given the size of the private area of the beach that had been cordoned off for the wedding reception. Stef decided to give up even trying.

She looked to where the steel drum band had set up their instruments and once again caught Dustin staring at her. When she didn't immediately look away, he apparently took it as permission to approach.

He strolled barefoot through the sand, his hands shoved into the pockets of the bone-colored linen pants he and the other groomsmen had worn for the ceremony. The tail end of his collarless white shirt blew in the gentle breeze coming off the ocean.

He stopped a couple of feet in front of her, but her body still heated from his nearness. Several moments drifted by before he finally spoke, his voice soft, but edged with a note of cautious humor.

"Are you still mad at me?"

"Yes," Stef answered.

He dipped his head until they were eye-level with each other. "You didn't have a problem with me before you knew that Stefan and I were friends," he said, his tone more earnest than amused. "Why does it have to change now?"

"Because you lied to me. Why didn't you just tell me who you really were?"

"The truth?"

She propped a fist on the fabric that gathered at the hip of her crinkled chiffon dress and continued to stare at him.

He blew out an exasperated breath. "Fine. I didn't say anything because I figured the minute you discovered that I wasn't just some random guy, you would clam up on me, and I didn't want our night to end. I was enjoying myself too much."

She would not allow his sweet words or the adorable contriteness in his eyes to sway her. She was stronger than that.

"When did you realize I was Stefan's sister?" she asked.

"When you mentioned that you were an army nurse," he admitted. "I should have known the moment you told me your name. Hell, I should have known just by looking at you. It's amazing how much you can look like him, yet still be so damn gorgeous."

Stef felt a blush creeping up her neck. Damn

him.

She looked toward the last rays of the sun setting over the water. "You can keep that flattery. It's not going to work on me."

"Oh, come on," he said, amusement shimmering in his voice. "It's my best asset." Two of his fingers caught her chin and turned her face toward him. "Are you really still upset?"

"Yes. I don't like being lied to." Despite her efforts to curb it, she felt a grin forming. "But give me a few minutes. There's a possibility I'll get over it."

The smile that gradually slid over his lips was both devastating and disarming. Stefanie had a feeling that he only brought it out when he really needed help getting out of the doghouse. It was working.

He wrapped his arms around her waist, his fingers resting lightly at the small of her back. Together they swayed to the mellow timbre of the steel drums.

"I apologize for not saying anything," he said. "I swear I wasn't trying to deceive you, but I didn't want to scare you off. If you knew who I was, you would have thanked me for that drink and that would have been the end of it. Admit it."

"It would have," she said, unable to deny the truth in that. "You were supposed to be a one-night thing. Even though, in the end we didn't do anything, just imagine how humiliated I would be today if something *had* happened between us?"

"Why would you be humiliated? There's nothing wrong with what we did last night. And even if we'd done more, it wouldn't have been anything you should be ashamed of. We're both single." He tipped her chin up. "And, just in case you were wondering, I would be more than willing to try again tonight."

Stef slapped his hand, even as need drizzled down her spine. "I told you that last night was a one-time thing. It was a silly dare. I've never been good at backing away from a dare."

"Is that so? Well." He leaned forward and whispered in her ear, "I dare you to leave this reception this instant and come up to my room with me."

"Save it. It's not going to work."

"I double-dog dare you."

She pushed away from him. "I give up."

"Okay, okay," he said, tugging her back into his arms. "I'll be serious."

"Are you even capable of being serious?"

"Only when the Colorado Rockies make it to the post-season, or when mercury is in retrograde."

She rolled her eyes.

"Being serious all the time is highly overrated," he said. "You said last night that you wanted to have some fun while you're on vacation. If you want fun, I'm your man."

She was so tempted. God, was she tempted.

She didn't know much about Dustin "Hawk" Patrick, but one thing she *did* know was how he made her feel when she was with him. She'd felt alive last night. She'd felt like the Stefanie she used to be—the fearless, fun-loving girl who wasn't afraid to let her hair down and enjoy life.

She wanted this. She wanted him. She wanted to feel like that girl just one more time before reality bombarded her when she returned to work on Tuesday morning.

"What do you say, Stefanie? You're here until Monday, right? Let me show you a good time."

Say yes!

But before she could say anything, the photographer came over and instructed them to meet at the head table for the wedding toast and cake cutting.

Maybe it was for the best that his question went unanswered. As much as she missed the reckless abandon that once epitomized her existence, she could never forget the cost when that recklessness finally caught up to her. She glanced quickly at her father; whose censure always served as a relentless reminder of that long ago incident that had changed everything.

She could not allow Dustin, or anyone else, to lead her down that path again. In the end, she would only regret it.

Dustin stood at the edge of the linen-draped bamboo tent that had been constructed on the beach to shield the reception guests from the brisk night-wind blowing off the ocean. He cradled a glass of bourbon in one hand while the other, out of habit, rubbed the spot on his hip where a crescent-shaped scar resided, a parting gift from his last week of combat in Afghanistan. The scar had become an odd sort of security blanket, the anchor he turned to when he needed to ruminate on something weighing on his mind.

Over the past few months, questions surrounding Hawk Offshore Transportation had sent him seeking comfort in that tangible reminder of how difficult life can be. The ridged line of knotted flesh never failed to put whatever was troubling him into perspective. In the grand scheme of things, he was lucky. A knick here, a scratch there, and a company worth millions. Yeah, he was lucky.

However, tonight's pondering had nothing to do with his company and everything to do with the woman standing several yards away, the gauzy fabric of her light-green dress billowing in the breeze.

He studied Stefanie's profile as she stood next to her new sister-in-law, toasting Callie and

Stefan on their marriage. No matter how hard he'd fought the urge to seek her out during the wedding and reception, Dustin couldn't stop his gaze from roaming to locate her.

From the moment she'd left him in his room last night, hot, bothered and in need of a cold shower, he'd been terrified of how things would play out when she discovered that he was Stefan's friend and boss. He'd figured she would be pissed, but he'd been floored at how quickly she seemed to have forgiven him.

Whether her forgiveness meant that she'd want anything to do with him after tonight was another question, but at least they were headed in the right direction.

Stefanie was that rare combination that had eluded him for much of his life—funny, sexy, daring, sensitive, and brave. She had a fire burning in her spirit that called to him. It was the same fire that burned in him. He'd sensed it from the moment he sat down next to her.

She wanted their time together to be limited to those few hours they'd shared yesterday and tonight. Dustin wasn't willing to accept that. Even though he probably should if he wanted to preserve a semblance of a relationship with his best friend.

Stefan had been on the verge of calling him out when he thought that Stefanie had spent the night in his bed, but Dustin had grown up fighting his two older brothers. He could take a good lick as well as dish a few out.

He wasn't going to fight his friend. Because Stefan knew the kind of man Dustin was, and even though he wouldn't admit it, he knew that Dustin was good enough for his sister.

Now, he just had to figure out how to make Stefanie see that he was good for her too. The spark between them had been too instantaneous, too electric. He wasn't sure if this was meant to last more than just this weekend; all he knew was that he had to have more of her.

She looked over at him and their gazes connected. After a brief pause to talk to her parents, she walked over to him. The fact that she sought him out this time gave Dustin just the shot of hope he needed.

"They look happy," he said, motioning toward Stefan and Callie.

She nodded as she wrapped a filmy shawl around her arms. "They're good for each other. They *get* each other. It's rare to find that."

"I understand," Dustin said. "How many times do you find two people who can talk about the most mundane things for hours and not get bored? Two people who share so many of the same interests, taste in fritters and Kool-Aid notwithstanding."

She laughed softly, but shook her head. "Don't Dustin. I told you, last night was a one-time thing."

"But it doesn't have to be." He captured her

hands between his. "You asked me if I knew how to be serious, and I'm telling you right now that I do. I'm being completely serious with you, Stefanie. Yesterday had nothing to do with you being Stefan's sister. Nothing. Once I figured out who you were, I tried to leave."

Surprise flashed in her eyes.

"I tried," he repeated, "because I knew your brother would be upset. But it didn't matter. None of it mattered, because the time we spent together yesterday was some of the most relaxing, enjoyable hours I've had in years. *Years*, Stefanie."

He tipped her chin up and stared into her eyes. "We both have one more day here in Turks and Caicos. I think it would be a crime if we didn't spend it together."

She pulled her bottom lip between her teeth. "I don't know."

"It's one day. All I'm asking for is one more day with you," Dustin lied. He wanted so much more, but he would cross the bridge of really pursuing her once they returned to Louisiana. "You said you wanted to prove to your friend that you haven't become a dull, boring stick-in-the-mud."

"A dull, boring stick-in-the-mud is a bit harsh," she said with a quick laugh.

"So prove that you're not one," he said. "Think of all the fun, adventurous things to do on this island. Spend the day with me tomorrow.

Let's make the most of our last day here."

She shook her head.

"Wait a minute," Dustin said. "I know how to make you say yes."

Her eyes narrowed. "Don't say it," Stefanie warned.

A wicked smile curved up the corners of his lips.

"I dare you."

"I don't know about this, Dustin."

"Oh, come on. *This* is too wild and crazy? A dune buggy?" Dustin didn't try to mask the incredulousness in his voice, but Stef didn't care. These things could be dangerous if you weren't careful. She walked around the low-sitting open-air vehicle while Dustin signed the paperwork relieving the rental company of any liability.

"You already chickened out of going cliff diving, even though you said you never back down from a dare," he pointed out.

She peered at him over the rim of her sunglasses. "There is a difference between taking on a dare and being a complete fool. I'm a nurse. I've seen my share of serious injuries, and anyone who dives off a cliff into a choppy ocean is just begging for a cracked clavicle. The same with these things. There's not even a cage holding us in."

Dustin responded with a fake yawn.

"Whatever." Stef laughed. She stuck her tongue out at him, eliciting a roguish grin that tickled all of her female parts. He was sexy even when he wasn't trying to be; it drizzled over him like honey down a honeycomb.

He inspected the vehicle's thick tires before accepting the keys from the rental company operator.

"So, are you chickening out of this, too?" he asked once he joined her again.

"When you said something adventurous I thought it would be a hike or something."

"You're army. You've parachuted from a plane. I would think you could handle riding along the beach in a glorified go-cart."

Dustin narrowed the distance between them, dipping his head slightly so that he could whisper in her ear. "I thought you army peeps were supposed to be fearless."

He was so close Stef could smell the resort's bath soap on his skin. Her eyes closed as she soaked in the maddening scent of citrus and man. She had to fight the urge to bury her face against his neck and snatch a taste of the magic she'd experienced Friday night when she'd held him against the door to his room.

Why do I have to want you so much?

Stef feared she already knew exactly why this man, whom she'd only known for a few days, elicited such a powerful response from her. He called to that girl who still lived deep inside. That wild, thrill-seeking, risk-taking girl who used to get off on pushing the limits and living on the edge. She'd spent years suppressing those urges — even through her adrenalin-packed army days — but one little taste of that remembered excitement had her craving it. And craving him.

Stef knew she could never fully embrace the wild child she used to be. Reality would hit her as soon as her plane touched the tarmac in Louisiana tomorrow. But she'd be damned if she wasn't going to enjoy it for today.

"What do you say, Stefanie? Are you ready for your adventure?" Dustin asked.

"There is only one way I'm getting into this dune buggy," she said. His brow quirked in inquiry. "I drive."

"*You're* going to drive?"

"That's right," Stef said, crossing her arms over her chest. If she drove, she could control the danger level and make sure things didn't get out of hand.

With a skeptical smirk curling the edges of his lips, he reluctantly held the keys out to her. "Fine. Just remember you're not driving Miss Daisy. You'd better put this baby through its paces."

Stef snatched the keys from his fingers, eager to wipe that grin off his handsome face.

Twenty minutes later, both she and Dustin

were screaming as the dune buggy went airborne over a rugged patch of vegetation. They splashed through a shallow creek, bumbling over the smooth, slippery rock bed.

"Damn, girl!" Dustin gripped the metal beam over his right shoulder. "You trying to give me a heart attack?"

"What's wrong, Miss Daisy? A little too wild for you?"

His full-on smile nearly knocked the air from her lungs. Giving him up at the end of the day was going to be *so* hard.

They drove through the island's salinas, the natural pools that were once used to collect salt from the ocean water. Following a map Dustin had taken from the dune buggy rental company's reception area, they made their way to the northern edge of the island, which was home to one of its most famous and historic sites, the Grand Turk Lighthouse.

They parked the dune buggy and started for the towering structure. "Can we go inside?" Stef asked.

"The map says that there are no inside tours, but we shouldn't let that stop us."

"Forget it. I'm not breaking into a lighthouse," Stef said.

Dustin let out an exasperated sigh. "I forgot. You're a goody-two-shoes army vet."

"Whatever." She laughed. "As if the navy is so badass."

"Navy is nothing but badass."

He took her by the hand as they walked along the grassy knoll surrounding the lighthouse. From this vantage point they could see some of the most amazing views of the ocean she'd ever experienced in her life.

For this brief moment in time, everything seemed perfect.

Stef tried not to lose sight of what this was—one day with him. That's all it was. She would not get swept up in the romance of this idyllic setting, or how strong and warm and soothing his palm felt against hers, or how easy he was to talk to about anything and everything. It was *one* day, so she'd better soak in the experience while she had the chance.

"My seven-year-old would love this," she said as she looked up at the cast-iron lighthouse painted in white. "He's so into history right now."

"Where is he?" Dustin asked.

"His grandparents—my late husband's mom and dad," she explained. "They retired to Florida, and they are determined to make my son overdose on theme parks over the next few weeks."

"Nonstop rollercoasters? Sounds like heaven on earth."

"Really?" She looked at him over her shoulder. "I would think a daredevil like you would fall asleep on rollercoasters. Just not exciting enough."

His deep chuckle rumbled through her, causing her belly to quake with want. She'd met him less than forty-eight hours ago, yet she was already starting to crave the sound of his voice.

"Does he visit them often?" Dustin asked. "Jacob, that's his name, right?"

"Yeah," Stef said, "and I've only just started to let him visit for extended periods of time. He's only seven, after all, but I know that having him there brings Robert and Shelia a bit of comfort. They both have had a hard time dealing with Brandon's death."

The last thing Stef wanted intruding on their day together was talk of her deceased husband, but it wasn't something they could ignore either.

"I'm sure it's been hard on you too," Dustin said, his voice cautiously low. "I mean, I don't know all the details, only what Stefan's shared."

"It's been an adjustment." Stef nodded. "I never imagined myself being a widow and single mother in my early thirties."

She turned back toward the ocean and studied the gentle waves kissing the shoreline.

"I think back on that last morning," she continued. "When Brandon left for work. He pulled out of the driveway fifteen minutes earlier than usual because he wanted to stop at the dry cleaners to complain about a tiny hole they'd burned into one of his suit coats. I often wonder if he'd still be here if he'd left at his normal time."

Dustin remained silent, his expression so empathetic that it made her chest ache with gratitude. Eventually, in that same soft, understanding voice, he asked, "How has Jacob handled it?"

"He misses him. At first he asked a lot of questions, but then, that's Jacob." A small smile drifted across her lips. "My son has a very old soul. We've had some interesting talks over my famous fried peanut-butter-and-banana sandwiches."

Dustin's face scrunched up. "Wait a minute. What?"

"You know. Elvis's favorite snack. It's like a grilled cheese, but with peanut butter and banana instead of cheddar."

"First of all, everyone knows that you use American cheese to make a grilled cheese, not cheddar. And fried peanut butter and bananas just sounds nasty."

"That's because you've never tried it," she said. "According to Jacob, I can open my own restaurant and serve nothing else, and make loads of money."

Dustin sauntered up to her, stopping a hairsbreadth away. "If that's the case, maybe you should make one of your famous sandwiches for me once we get back home."

He ran a single finger down her cheek, then back up. Stefanie's eyelids slid shut, the ache that had settled in her chest taking on new meaning.

"I already told you, Dustin. We can't see each other once I'm back in Maplesville."

"Why are you so anxious to see this end?" The pained rasp in his voice only added to the sudden hurt crowding her chest. "Can you honestly tell me you have no problem with never seeing me again after today?"

"Dustin..."

"This doesn't have to be the end, Stefanie. It doesn't have to be anything too heavy either. It can just be what it has been this weekend, two people getting to know each other better, enjoying each other's company, pretending they both aren't turned on as hell by that kiss the other night."

The backs of his fingers dusted lightly across her jaw. His soft, warm lips followed. He traced a path along her skin, his nose nudging along the curve of her neck. He sucked in a deep breath.

"We've been in the sun all day. How can you still smell so amazing," he whispered as his nose traveled further down her neck.

A hushed gasp escaped Stef's mouth at the feel of the openmouthed kiss he pressed against her skin. He drew a trail of moist kisses along her jawline, then cupped her cheeks and brought her lips to his.

Whatever pittance of resistance she still

possessed melted the moment his tongue touched hers. With tender insistence he eased his way into her mouth, moving with long, lush strokes. Desire swirled within her belly, slowly building with every languid caress of his tongue.

Stef ran her hands up his back, while Dustin's trailed down her sides, stopping at her hips. His fingers spanned her sides, pressing lightly into her backside. He pulled her in closer, fitting her body against his. The sensation lit a fire within her, its flames licking at her nerve endings, causing her nipples to pebble with need and the spot between her legs to grow wet with want.

This is what she had been missing. This heady feeling of being desired, of being transported to a distant world where the only thing that existed was pleasure. She missed this. She *needed* this. She wanted to feel this over and over and over again, until her entire body was nothing but a mass of pulsating sensations.

Dustin continued his brutally sensual assault on her mouth, pressing his tongue harder and deeper, doing the same with his body. Stef welcomed every delicious thrust, her own tongue seeking, devouring, until she thought she would die from the pleasure of it.

When their mouths finally broke apart, she had to take a moment to get her bearings. His kiss had left her knees weak, her mind tangled.

"My God, Stefanie." Dustin pressed his

forehead against hers, his breaths labored as they soughed in and out of his mouth. "If you even try to tell me you don't want this, I'm calling you a damn liar."

"I never said I didn't want it." She captured the fingers that continued to trail along her cheek and looked him in the eye. "But it doesn't change anything. I can't be this same woman back in Louisiana."

His pained expression tore a hole in her heart.

"I'm sorry, Dustin." Her voice came out raspy as she tried to recover from that kiss. "This weekend was exactly what I needed, but it has to be just that. Just this weekend."

He cupped her face and pulled her closer to him. "You're making a mistake," he said. "From what I can tell you need some fun in your life. I can provide that. Your fun doesn't have to stay here on Grand Turk."

His thumb brushed faintly across the tiny scar behind her ear.

Stef jerked her head back. Feeling his soft touch against the physical reminder that remained from her long ago mistake had the impact of being doused with a bucket of ice water.

She sucked in a deep breath and slowly exhaled.

"I just can't," she said. "Please, don't let this ruin the rest of our day together," she pleaded.

"I need...I need you to be okay with this, even if you have to pretend. We only have a few hours left. I want us to enjoy them."

A muscle flexed in his stubble-covered jaw, but after a moment his face relaxed. He even gifted her with a soft, slightly resigned smile.

"Fine," he said. "But to show you just how big a mistake you're making, I'm even going to let you continue to drive. See the kind of man you're giving up?"

Stef couldn't help but laugh. It really would be hard to give him up.

But she would. She had to.

By the time they returned to the rental place, Stef's legs were caked with mud, and her hands ached from her vise grip on the steering wheel. She didn't care if her hands hurt for a week, nothing could make her regret the past couple of hours. Adrenalin pumped through her veins, wild and brilliant and exhilarating.

"I can't remember the last time I had this much fun."

"I think you're in the wrong profession," Dustin said. "NASCAR drivers make a helluva lot more than nurses. You'd kick ass on the circuit."

"Admit it." She nudged him with her shoulder. "This was better than cliff diving."

"I don't know about that," he said. "If we were cliff diving, I would get to see you in a bikini."

"Who says I would have worn a bikini?"

"Don't ruin my fantasy."

"I'm not sure I wanted to know that you've been fantasizing about my swimwear."

He lolled his head to the side and hit her with the most delectably wicked grin. "In my mind it's red, with ruffles along the edges and skinny little strings holding it together."

Stef thought about the plain navy-blue one-piece in her suitcase and burst out laughing. "You would be *so* disappointed with the bathing suit I packed."

"I think I should be the judge of that."

"Nice try, but you're not getting me in a swimsuit today."

He grumbled as he climbed out of the dune buggy. He pointed to a water hose next to the building. "Looks like we can wash off over there."

As they started toward the building, Stef said, "There's something that's been niggling at me since yesterday morning when I found out you were Stefan's Hawk."

"Stefan's Hawk? Makes me sound like a pet."

"You know what I mean," she said. "Anyway, I'm trying to figure out how is it that we're meeting each other for the first time in Turks and Caicos? Stefan's been working for you for over a year now."

"Yeah, but I only moved to Louisiana a few

months ago," he said as he used the water hose to wash the mud from her legs. His large, steady palm moved efficiently up and down her calves, loosening the caked on dirt.

He peered up at her, his eyes crinkling at the corners. "You're getting turned on, aren't you?"

"Shut up." Stefanie laughed. She refused to admit that he was right. Having his hands on her, even in this detached way, excited her to the point of making her skin hot.

"You've been running your company remotely all this time?" she asked, getting back to her original question.

"It isn't that hard to do." He stood, rinsed off his fingers, and wiped them dry on his tank top. "I've got some good men and women working for me. They were able to handle things as I moved the base of operations from Alaska south to the Gulf. It was the best decision I've ever made. I grew up in Denver, but nothing in Colorado prepared me for that Alaska cold. It's brutal."

"So you traded the bitter cold for scorching Louisiana summers."

He shrugged. "Louisiana just has a lot more to offer — good food, great fishing, and as I recently discovered, some of the sexiest ER nurses you will ever find."

Stef could feel the blush climbing up her cheeks. "You are an impossible flirt. I don't know how people put up with you."

"And yet here you are, putting up with me. Why is that?"

Why? Was that really a question? Why *wouldn't* she want to spend her day enjoying a gorgeous man's flattery?

"I'll tell you why," Dustin continued, his body closing in on hers. "It's because underneath that ponytail and those shorts that are too damn long, a part of you likes it. Admit it, Stefanie. It's that same part of you that was ready to have a one-night stand with me on Friday."

Heat flooded her bloodstream, but Stef refused to give him the satisfaction of knowing that he read her so accurately. She folded her arms across her chest and jutted her chin in the air. "I didn't go through with it."

He pressed his lips against her ear, and whispered, "But you wanted to."

Oh yes.

Her body mourned the loss of what she could have experienced if only she had remained in his room. Any man who could be so in tune to what she was thinking would be that much more perceptive to what her body needed.

Stef knew she would question the wisdom of not allowing him free rein over her body for a long, *long* time to come.

"You don't have to admit you like me," Dustin said. "It'll just make me work harder to prove it."

"I never said I didn't like you."

"But you still won't see me after today?"

She hated to hurt him, but if it took saying it in no uncertain terms to finally get the point across, that's what she had to do.

"That's right," Stef said. "I won't see you after today.

Chapter Three

Dustin drummed his pen against the stack of papers crowding his desk as he reread the latest e-mail from Global Offshore Drilling. It had arrived in his inbox while he and Stefanie were traipsing around Grand Turk in a dune buggy. He'd read and reread it in the five days since they'd flown back to Louisiana, but had yet to respond.

Global wasn't the first company to offer to buy him out, but they sure as hell were the most aggressive. At first the e-mails would pop up every couple of months. Then they started coming monthly and finally weekly, until they were getting harder to ignore. The latest e-mail came complete with bullet points, laying out everything that he would gain if he finally caved to the pressure the bigger company had been exerting on him to sell.

Unlike the previous offers, this one included something extra—a deadline. Global wanted an answer in thirty days or they would seek out another "viable shuttle service to add to their offshore drilling outfit."

Thirty days.

He had less than a month to decide whether

to keep the dream he'd built out of nothing or sell his business, acquiring in a single transaction enough money to last him a lifetime.

The money doesn't matter.

At least, that's what Dustin kept repeating over and over in his head. Maybe if he said it enough he could ignore the trail of zeros in Global's e-mail. The company had upped their previous bid by more than twelve percent, bringing it to a cool eighty million dollars.

It was one reason why Dustin had studied this e-mail so much longer than the others. After a while, he'd started deleting the messages as soon as they hit his inbox, but this time Global's lawyer had been cagey enough to put the dollar figure in the subject line. Eighty million dollars was enough to give anybody pause.

It held even greater significance for him because it was the perfect revenge.

Selling Hawk Transpo for eighty million would prove that he was a success to all those people who only equated success with dollar signs, like his two older brothers. He shouldn't *have* to prove anything to them, but dammit, he *wanted* to.

Dustin had always gotten off on doing the impossible, on proving people wrong, especially Sidney and Sean, his bigger, badder older brothers. Neither thought their scrawny book-nerd younger brother, with an IQ outside of this stratosphere, could make it as a navy pilot, but for six years Dustin kicked ass and took names in that Hawkeye.

Once he left the navy, in his siblings' minds, it was a foregone conclusion that he would get a desk job in some nice, safe glass-and-concrete skyscraper, or—as his mother had hoped—go back to school to become a professor. Everyone was so certain that he'd gotten this crazy need to fly out of his system. No more planes or helicopters for Dustin.

So, what had he done? He'd bought a fleet of them. With a few savvy investments and a bit of luck, he'd turned his small idea into one of the fastest-growing shuttle services in the oil and gas industry.

He just had not anticipated *how* fast Hawk Transpo would grow, or that the more successful the company became, the less he would enjoy coming in to work every day.

That had been the biggest shocker in all of this. It wasn't until he realized that he was spending most of his days and much of his nights negotiating contracts, catching up on the latest health and safety regulations, and mitigating the everyday crises that tended to pop up that Dustin recognized that he was no longer having fun.

He knew better than to think of life as one big party, but he'd never intended to spend all of his time stuck behind a desk. He'd become jealous of his own pilots. They were the ones who saw all the action. The most action he saw was a quick flight to some oil company's downtown headquarters.

Which was why he should welcome the fact that companies like Global Offshore Drilling were breathing down his neck. They could take away the burdens that continued to weigh him down, burdens he hadn't anticipated when he'd started on this adventure. Not only that, the prospect of retiring at thirty-five years old with millions in the bank just could not be ignored.

But he always came back to his employees and the commitment he'd made to them. Hawk Transpo had a purpose that went beyond just making money. He couldn't sell out the ideals behind his business for easy cash.

"But eighty mil?" Dustin turned away from the computer screen and scrubbed both hands down his face. He knew ignoring this issue wouldn't make it go away. Even if he managed to hold off Global Offshore, it wouldn't be long before another company started filling his in-box and voice mail with buyout offers.

He guessed this is what people meant when they said they've become a victim of their own success.

He picked up the other thick contract he'd needed to read over since before his trip to Grand Turk. He was close to sealing the deal with a drilling company out of Galveston that had just finished their third deep-water rig in the

Gulf of Mexico. If this deal went as planned, he would be able to bring in two additional pilots — veterans of war who were making their way back into civilian life, like every other pilot on his staff.

Better than anyone else, a fellow veteran understood the hardships of returning from a deployment. It wasn't easy to slide back into civilian life, especially for those who did multiple tours. Finding rewarding work was even more difficult.

Many companies were doing the right thing — actively seeking veterans to employ — but Dustin went beyond just seeking. He made it Hawk Transpo's mission to hire veterans. Not only did he give them a job, but he provided whatever he could to help them succeed in other aspects of their lives. Mental health resources, relationship counseling, financial help by way of low-interest personal loans — whatever they needed.

And that was the rub with Global Offshore Drilling — with *any* of the conglomerates that had shown interest in purchasing his company. How would he know if the new buyer would honor the pledge he'd made to support and employ veterans? How could he know if they would continue providing these much-needed services that he made a priority?

If he sold, Dustin would have zero say in how the company operated. Was eighty million dollars in his own pocket and proving his brothers wrong, worth it if it meant his employees—men and women who were like family to him—might suffer because of him?

With a frustrated curse, Dustin tossed the contract on his desk. Thinking about this shit was giving him a headache.

He knew he couldn't continue putting this stuff off indefinitely. *But I don't have to do it right now.*

If he were going to give himself heartburn, he'd much prefer it be at the hands of a certain ER nurse who had made a sport out of evading him.

Dustin grabbed his cellphone. He knew full well he was setting himself up for more disappointment, but that hadn't stopped him the last ten times he'd texted Stefanie since they'd returned from the wedding.

She'd lived up to her vow to avoid him. She hadn't been nasty in her brush-offs, had even included a couple of smiley faces in her texts. But a rejection accompanied by a smiley face was still a rejection, and each rebuff just compelled Dustin to try harder.

He tapped the phone against his lips, contemplating which tactic he would try today. A grin broke out over his face as he pounded out a message:

Don't mean to bother you. Just wanted to know if you could tell me where I could get a fried banana and

---

peanut butter sandwich.

He pressed SEND and waited for a reply. And waited. And waited.

The sinking feeling that was becoming all too familiar started to settle in his gut.

Why was she giving him such a hard time? That there was chemistry between them was undeniable. Dustin wouldn't be surprised if they had left burn marks in the sand near the lighthouse in Grand Turk, that's just how electric the connection had been. Why was she so adamant that their time together be limited to those few days on the islands?

Just as he set the phone back onto his desk it chimed with the arrival of a text.

Sorry. Only know of my kitchen, and I only make fried PB and banana sandwiches for my favorite guy.

Fireworks exploded in Dustin's chest. This was the longest text he'd gotten from her since they'd returned to Louisiana.

Aw. C'mon, Dustin typed. *Jacob wouldn't mind you sharing his fave food with me.*

A full minute passed before she responded. *I'm working. Make your own sandwich.*

I need you to show me how to do it.

Now I get it. That's why you and Stefan are such good friends. Both helpless in the kitchen.

She had him smiling so hard his damn cheeks hurt.

Dustin's thumbs flew across the touchscreen. *I'm willing to take your abuse because I really want that sandwich. I can wait until your shift ends.*

This time the reply was instant. *I get off in a half-hour.*

He had to stop himself from replying in all caps. *Great! See you soon!*

Dustin hopped up from behind his desk so fast he sent the chair sailing into the wall behind him. He stopped at Jaycee Miller's desk just long enough to let his self-described receptionist, office manager, and all-around rock star know that he was leaving for the day.

Dustin took the stairs two at a time, reaching the landing pad on the roof of the fifty-thousand-square-foot warehouse he'd purchased in Belle Chase eighteen months ago. He jumped into the R22 Beta two-seater helicopter, one of three that he kept for quick flights, and twenty minutes later landed at the remote end of the parking lot at Maplesville General Hospital.

"What are you smiling about?"

Stefanie looked up from the open gash she was cleaning to find the charge nurse, Angelica Reynolds, standing just inside the exam room's curtained area.

"What was that?" Stef asked.

"I don't know about you," Angelica said as

she sauntered toward her. "But debriding a wound usually doesn't put a smile on my face. I wanna know what's put this one on yours."

Stef rolled her eyes, but as much as she tried to fight it she couldn't prevent the smile from climbing across her lips again. "Can't a person just smile?"

"Nope." Angelica snapped on a pair of latex gloves and bumped Stef with her hip. "Get out of here. You're off duty."

"That's okay. I can finish this up."

The charge nurse hit her with one of her lethal stares.

"Okay, okay." Stef's hands shot up in surrender. "You don't have to tell me twice. The wound is yours." She turned to the patient. "Remember what I said, Darius, if you're going to hike in those woods, you have to be careful of hunting traps. This could have ended much worse for you."

"Yes, ma'am," the high schooler answered.

Stef set the surgical scissors on the tray and thanked Angelica again before heading to her locker to change out of her nursing scrubs. She tried her best to ignore the heightened anticipation humming through her belly as she pulled the fitted t-shirt over her head and zipped up her snug dark-blue jeans. She'd bought both during an impromptu lunch stop at the outlet mall.

Stef closed her locker and leaned her head

against it.

What was she doing? She knew better than this. Encouraging Dustin was akin to letting a caged tiger loose in her world. But *he* wasn't the tiger—*she* was. He called to that part of her she'd tried so hard to suppress. He stoked that banked fire within her, seducing the inner wild child who had nearly cost her everything she'd held dear.

She'd given herself those few days with him in Turks and Caicos. That should have been the end of it. But for the past five days, Stef had been hard-pressed to think of anything but him.

So she told herself that she would give him these remaining two weeks until Jacob returned from his grandparents. Once her son was back at home, she would go back to being the responsible adult she'd cultivated over this past decade.

As for now, she would enjoy this exciting man who'd come into her life.

She spun the combination on her lock, and after a quick glance in the mirror to swipe on lip gloss and tighten her ponytail holder, she headed out of the employee locker room.

"You're still smiling," Angelica said as Stef passed her in the corridor.

She secretly enjoyed the fact that she was driving her nosy co-workers crazy with her odd behavior. They were not used to seeing this side of her.

It's not as if she always walked around with a frown on her face, but it was common knowledge that she'd had very little to smile about this past year — these past couple of years really.

Losing her husband unexpectedly in a car accident had tilted her world off its axis. Being called to serve a six-month tour in Afghanistan not even a year later had further rumbled the shaky ground she'd been standing on. If not for the sheer joy Jacob brought to her life simply by existing, and the steadiness she found in her job here at Maplesville General, she wouldn't have had anything at all to smile about.

That had changed over the course of this past week. She'd found herself grinning often since she returned from Grand Turk. Just the thought that she would soon see the man who'd given her a new reason to smile made her skin tingle in anticipation.

She had just rounded the hallway toward the ER's exit when the automatic doors opened and Dustin walked through them. Dark aviator sunglasses shaded his eyes, and sexiness dripped off of him like he'd cornered the market on male hotness. Her steps faltered as he strode toward her looking like a Hollywood actor in an action/adventure film.

"Perfect timing," he said. His eyes coasted from the top of her head to her toes. "Damn, you look amazing. Has it really been less than a week since I last saw you?"

Two seconds and he was already flirting.

"How did you get here so quickly?" Stef asked.

His shoulders lifted in a casual shrug as he hooked the sunglasses to the collar of his black polo shirt. "Helicopter."

"You actually *flew* here from Belle Chase? Who travels by helicopter?"

Another shrug. "A guy who owns a fleet of them. I hate being on the road with people who are too busy checking their Facebook statuses to watch where they're going. Birds are so much easier to deal with."

Her lips tilted in a grin. "I guess you don't have to worry about birds using Facebook."

"Nah, they use Twitter." He winked. "Get it?"

Her loud crack of laughter turned several heads in the ER waiting room. "What am I going to do with you?"

The gleam in his eyes was so wicked it made her face heat. "I have so many suggestions," he said, his voice dropping several octaves. "However, you can start out by feeding me a peanut butter and banana sandwich. We can talk about those other ideas once we've both had a little sustenance."

Shivers shuttled down her spine as a throng of naughty thoughts flooded her brain. She could only imagine the kind of ideas he would suggest. The man was trouble—the most incredibly perfect kind of trouble.

"So… about that sandwich?" he asked, dangling his keys.

"It's probably better that we take my car," Stef said. "You'd look kind of silly filing a flight plan to my house."

His eyes flashed with amusement. "As long as I'm not flying in restricted airspace I don't have to file a flight plan. We won't break any laws by taking my ride."

"Ah, well, my driveway isn't big enough to park *your ride*."

"But just think of how cool a helicopter would make you look to all your neighbors. Mad street cred."

Laughing again—it was truly amazing how easily he made her do that—Stef caught him by the wrist and tugged him out the door to her metallic blue Chevy Traverse. As they made the short ten-minute drive to the cozy home she and Brandon bought when they moved to Maplesville, Stef tried her hardest to squelch the combination of fear, excitement, and exhilaration churning in her stomach.

This was only until Jacob returned. She was having a little fun. There was nothing wrong with having a little fun, was there?

Dread seeped up her throat as she remembered the last time she'd said those words.

But she wasn't going back to being that girl again. She had more self-control than she'd had back in her wild and reckless days. She could let her hair down and enjoy this time with Dustin, and when it came time to end it, she would end it.

It was supposed to end when you left Grand Turk.

Stef quickly shut the lid on that thought. She *would* end it this time. This was only temporary fun.

The moment they entered the house, Sandy, Jacob's fat tabby cat, made her presence known. She rubbed against Stef's leg, the gray and white tail curling along her calf.

"Is this the infamous Sandy?" Dustin asked.

"How do you know about Sandy?"

"Everybody at Hawk Transpo knows about the cat that brought Stefan and Callie together. Sandy is our unofficial mascot."

She should have known her brother's friends and coworkers would know the story of how Stefan and Callie met. He'd brought Sandy into Callie's veterinary practice after he'd rescued her from the drainage ditch at the edge of Stef's property.

Dustin stooped down and scooped Sandy into his arms, running his hand along the cat's fur and melting every single inch of Stef's heart. Before this very moment Stef had had no idea that men who liked cats turned her on.

Apparently they did.

Sucking in a quick breath to calm her suddenly overactive heart, she clapped her hands together. "Why don't I get started on the sandwiches."

"You need any help?" Dustin asked.

"I've got it. Make yourself at home."

Stef sought the sanctuary of the kitchen and used the minutes it took to throw the sandwiches together to collect herself. She needed to find some control. She had been so close to sleeping with this man after knowing him for just a few hours. If she were not careful, she would drag him upstairs to her bedroom before they had the chance to eat.

"Do *not* do that," she warned herself in a low tone as she slid the sandwiches on separate plates.

When she returned to the living room, she found Dustin standing over the coffee table, studying the diorama she and Jacob had been working on for the past month.

"You've discovered my son's newest project," Stef said.

Dustin shot her a brief glance before returning his attention to the model. "I have no idea what this is, but it is cool as shit," he said as he walked around the table, Sandy still in his arms.

"It's the Chalmette Battlefield. Jacob's class visited it on a field trip this spring, and he became obsessed with the War of 1812. He was already obsessed with dioramas. He's built a few before, but nothing on this scale."

Dustin leaned in closer, his gaze intent as he studied each and every piece. "This is amazing. The kid has talent."

"I agree, but then, I'm biased." Stef laughed.

She set the plates on the bar that separated the kitchen and living room before joining him at the coffee table.

"Jacob is super-meticulous about everything he does. Every piece has to be perfect." She picked up the tiny blue cannon from the table. "I've been working on the cannons and the oak tree they sit under, but I want to make sure I have the proportions correct before I set them in place. I've searched for pictures online, but haven't been able to find just the right angle. I want to have it done by the time Jacob comes home as a surprise for him."

"When does he get back?"

"Not for another two weeks, but with my shift schedule there's no way I'll make it all the way out to Chalmette to see it for myself."

"Why don't we go right now?"

She jerked in surprise. "What?"

"After we eat we can head out there."

"No we can't."

"Why not?"

She somehow managed not to roll her eyes. "For one thing, the battlefield's visiting hours are during the day, which makes it pretty difficult since I work mostly the day shift. And, secondly, it's nearly an hour away."

The mischievous glint in his eyes sent a shot of both alarm and excitement down Stef's spine.

Dustin slowly shook his head. "Not if you travel by helicopter."

"Didn't you just hear me say that the battlefield is closed?"

His brow lifted with deliberate smugness. "You're not gonna let that stop you, are you?"

"You're insane," Stef said, even as she tried to halt the rush of adrenalin that coursed through her veins. "I'm not breaking into the Chalmette Battlefield."

"You really are a goody-two-shoes, aren't you?"

"Sticks and stones," Stef said.

"It would take twenty minutes to fly there in my helo."

"We cannot just land a helicopter at the Chalmette Battlefield and break in."

"Of course we can. Get your stuff together and let's go."

Stef crossed her arms over her chest. "I'm not doing it, Dustin."

His grin grew wider, and Stefanie knew then and there that she was in trouble. He sauntered over to her. With that devilish gleam still shining in his eyes, he leaned forward and whispered in her ear, "I dare you."

Chapter Four

"I must be out of my mind to let you talk me into doing this," Stefanie hissed in a harsh whisper.

A deep chuckle reverberated through Dustin's chest as he watched her crouch in the open pasture, her head turning from left to right and back again, her eyes wide and suspicious.

"Why are you stooping down?" he asked with a laugh. "Who do you expect to spot us? The ghost of Jean Lafittte?"

"Shhh." She batted her hand at him and yanked at his wrist. "Get down. There are probably guards walking the grounds. We're lucky if we don't get our heads shot off."

"Do you really think the state goes to the expense of hiring armed guards to patrol a two-hundred-year-old battlefield? Who would break in here?"

She slid a sardonic look his way.

"Well, except for the two of us," Dustin finished with a grin.

"I can*not* believe I let you talk me into this."

"Come here," he said, tightening his hand around hers. He tugged her from her crouched position and pulled her toward him. His thighs brushed against hers. The contact caused his breath to quicken.

"Think about it," Dustin said. "If we were going to get caught, it would have happened already. Someone would have called the police the minute they saw the helo land."

She did that frantic left-to-right-to-left thing again, as if she was watching a ping-pong match. Dustin captured her chin, steadying her head so that he could look her in the eye.

"Calm down, Stefanie." He tried to keep the amusement from his voice. He really, really did. But it wasn't working.

"Would you please stop making fun of me," she said. "Do you know how embarrassing it would be if we got arrested for breaking into a historical landmark? How would I explain that to my coworkers?"

"We won't get arrested." Dustin pressed his lips against her ear. "Just think of the look on Jacob's face when he comes home to find his diorama finished. That alone will be worth having an arrest for B&E on your record, won't it?"

He held his mouth in place for several heartbeats longer than necessary, breathing in her scent. He felt the slight shiver that ran through her body, and his followed in kind.

"You are nothing but trouble." Her husky tone only added fuel to the fire simmering in his bloodstream.

"But you like my kind of trouble," Dustin murmured against the curve of her jaw.

"I do," she said. "You have no idea how much I wish I didn't, but I do."

Dustin trailed his hands along her arms as he stepped in even closer, bringing his body flush against hers. "There's a lot more of this kind of trouble we can get into. Give me a chance and I'll have you craving it."

Her lids fluttered shut. She tipped her head back slightly, her lips poised in the perfect position to be kissed. But then she opened her eyes and said, "I know. That's what scares me."

She took a step back, rubbing her hands up and down her arms as if to ward off a chill.

Dustin's brow furrowed. "Stef—"

She put her hand up. "Let's...let's just go find what we came here for.

Unease curdled the warm feelings that had been swirling in his gut only a second ago. He didn't know what to make of the sharp change in her tone.

Dustin humored her, ducking his head and scurrying across the freshly mowed field. They arrived at the decrepit cannon, which sat underneath the arching branches of a mossy oak tree.

"Maybe we should have come when it was still light out," Dustin said. "You won't be able to take any good pictures in the dark."

"If we'd come before nightfall, we would

have been caught," Stef whispered. "And please lower your voice. They may not have anyone out here, but there may be someone in the house." She pointed to the large plantation home that stood on the property.

Peering at the cannon as if she was looking for the perfect shot, she took a couple of steps to the right and then let out a scream loud enough to wake the soul of every soldier who'd perished there in the Battle of New Orleans.

"Bug! Bug!" She hopped up and down like her feet were on fire, slapping at her legs with licks hard enough to leave handprints.

Dustin stared for several moments before he balled his fist over his gut and fell over laughing. He laughed so hard his side hurt. He had to take several huge gulps of air before he could get control over himself. Once he could finally stand without falling into another fit of laughter, he found Stefanie staring at him with her arms crossed. Apparently, she hadn't found it as amusing as he had.

"You about done?" she asked him.

He shook his head, wiping the tears of mirth that had collected at the corners of his eyes. "I think so," he managed to get out.

"You find my fear of bugs funny?"

"As hell," he said. "What happened to the big bad army girl? And you had the nerve to make fun of this navy man?"

She shook her head. "Just when I was

starting to like you."

She tried to turn away, but Dustin caught her by the shoulders. "I'm sorry for laughing at you."

"No, you're not." She swatted his hand.

"No, but why don't we just pretend that I am. It'll make it easier for both of us to move on."

Annoyance flashed in her eyes. "This isn't funny, Dustin. It's a real problem. My fear of bugs has caused serious issues in my relationship with my son."

Dustin sobered at the earnestness in her tone. "What kind of issues?"

"Jacob loves bugs. I have no idea why. I guess it's a boy thing."

"Sure, at that age boys like bugs," Dustin said.

"Yes, and I hate them, but I don't want Jacob to know that. So whenever he asks to go looking for lightning bugs or crickets or any of those other creepy-crawly things, I have to come up with an excuse because I'm too ashamed to let my son discover that his mom is total chicken shit."

Dustin's lips twitched. "You're not chicken shit," he said, smoothing a hand down her sleek ponytail.

Stefanie's head bobbed with a vigorous nod. "Oh, yes I am. When it comes to bugs of any kind, I am *total* chicken shit." She blew out a sigh. "It's not as if Jacob doesn't get to do all those boy things that he loves. Stefan has stepped in to help with stuff like that more times than I can count, but he's married now. I can't rely on Stefan forever."

"Your brother loves that little boy more than you can possibly know. He isn't leaving Jacob's life just because he and Callie got married."

"I know that," she said with another of those sighs. "But I don't want him to feel responsible for doing things with Jacob just because I'm not comfortable doing them myself. Who knows what the future holds for him and Callie. They may decide to have their own baby soon." She placed her palm to her chest. "Jacob is *my* son. After Brandon died, I accepted that I would have to be both mother and father to him. And that includes touching nasty little bugs if that's what my son wants us to do."

Her shoulders shook with exaggerated shivers, wresting another laugh from him. Dustin wasn't sure how to approach what he was about to say, so he just said it.

"I can do it." He put both hands up with a quick explanation. "I'm not trying to intrude or push. I just happen to think kids are cool. If you need someone to hang out with Jacob and do the kind of things you're not up to doing, maybe I can help."

Her eyes softened. "That's incredibly sweet of you to offer, but I can't expect you to step in."

He didn't have to ask why. He already knew.

During their quick flight over, she'd explained that their time together must be limited to the short couple of weeks that Jacob was away. Once he returned from visiting his grandparents, things would have to return to the way they were. Dustin had protested, but she'd been adamant.

It's a good thing he was always up for a challenge, because he wasn't about to give her up. Stefanie was what he had been looking for, that spark in his life that he knew was missing but couldn't put a name to. She was sweet, funny, sexy — *damn was she sexy* — and full of life. Dustin could not fathom going back to the way things were before he came upon her at that beach bar in Grand Turk.

The tricky part would be making *her* see that there was no going back.

"If I can't take Jacob out on his bug-hunting adventures, at least let me help you get over your fear so that you can," Dustin said.

She shook her head. "That will never happen. I've been this way since the fourth grade. Stefan hid this huge grasshopper under my pillow, and it hopped on my face while I was sleeping. I went to school the next day with a self-inflicted black eye."

Dustin nearly busted a vein trying to keep a straight face.

"Go ahead," she said.

He burst out laughing, once again wiping tears from his eyes.

"Boys are so dumb," Stefanie said with a snort as she stomped out of his reach.

Using the built-in flash on her phone, she snapped pictures of the cannon from every angle. She even walked several yards out and took shots of the tree, before declaring she had enough.

As they hiked back through the field on their way to the helicopter, Dustin was relentless in his teasing. He couldn't help it; she was too damn cute not to tease. He tickled her ear with a long blade of grass he'd snatched from the base of the tree. She jumped and swatted his hand away again.

"You're such a brat," she said with a laugh. "A sexy one, but still a brat."

"I'm just trying to help you get over your fear of bugs."

"By giving me a heart attack?"

"Actually, it's called systematic desensitization."

She stopped and turned. "What?"

"Uh, it's just this thing where you slowly expose someone to their fear until they finally get over it," he said with a shrug. This really wasn't the place to explain his massive IQ and how he was capable of digesting and storing tons of information in that brain of his.

Dustin snapped his fingers. "I have an idea. I know the perfect place we can go to help you get over your fear."

"Where's that?"

"If I tell you, then you probably wouldn't come." He helped her into the R22 and strapped her into the seat. "But I promise it will be worth your while."

Suspicion knitted her brow. "Does it involve breaking the law again?"

"Nope." Dustin shook his head. "We can go during regular business hours. Do you work weekends?"

"I'm covering for a friend tomorrow, but it's only a half-shift. I'll be done by one o'clock."

"How about I pick you up then?"

"In a car this time?"

He blew out an exasperated breath. "If you insist," he said.

He rounded the helo and climbed into the pilot seat. He handed her the hearing-protection headset before placing his own over his ears. He started up the bird, the whooping of the blades stirring the grass around them. "So," he asked. "What do you say?"

"If it means that I can eventually catch lightning bugs with my son, I'm in. You don't even have to dare me this time."

Stef held the six-year-old girl's arm steady as Dr. Sengupta fitted the plaster cast around her wrist. When the girl started to cry again, Stef tucked a blond curl behind her tiny ear and whispered, "You want to know what's neat about a cast? All of your friends at school can sign it. I still have my cast from when I broke my arm back in the seventh grade."

"How...how did you...break it," the little girl asked between hiccups.

"I was at a party at the skating rink. I fell and then someone rolled over my wrist."

"Ouch," Dr. Sengupta said.

Stef looked at him over the child's head and mouthed *not helping*.

"Sorry," the young doctor replied.

They finished setting the cast, and Stef gave the little girl's mother instructions on how to take care of her arm while the child was healing. She finished up the paperwork and brought it to the charge station.

"Skateboard?" Angelica asked.

"Jungle gym," Stef replied.

"Same difference. Both end in broken bones. An accident waiting to happen."

"I used to love the jungle gym when I was a kid," Stef said.

"You?" Angelica eyed her with a skeptical hitch of her brow. "You don't seem like the daredevil type."

Stef nearly choked on her laugh. She'd

apparently done a heck of a job in suppressing that inner wild child, seeing as she'd been the epitome of a daredevil up until her early twenties. She still wasn't sure if she was happy about having traveled so far to the other end of the spectrum, but she would always be grateful that she'd changed her ways before anything more catastrophic happened.

Well, more catastrophic than what actually *had* happened on this exact day twelve years ago.

Stef's eyes fell shut as she thought about Tania's phone call earlier this morning. After everything, her friend called every year on the anniversary to see if Stef was okay, when it should have been the other way around.

"Hey, I'm happy I caught you!"

Stef looked up and spotted Callie jogging toward her. Dressed in scrubs and a lab coat, she fit right in with the rest of the scenery, except for the dog and cat silhouette stitched above her name.

"Hey," Stef greeted. "What are you doing here?"

"Coming to beg my favorite sister-in-law for a favor," Callie said.

"I won't bother pointing out that I'm your only sister-in-law."

"Even if I had others, you'd still be my favorite."

"Uh oh." Stef laughed. "It must be a really

big favor."

Callie looked around. "Is there somewhere we can talk?"

"Sure." She guided her to a small alcove a few steps away from the charge station. "What's going on?"

"I need your help in surprising Stefan," she said. "Dustin is throwing us a party at his place. A reception for the friends and family who we couldn't invite to the wedding."

"Really? That's so sweet of him." How could that man melt her heart even when he wasn't trying? Although Stef found it strange that he hadn't mentioned anything yesterday.

"He just called me today with the idea," Callie said, as if answering Stef's mental question. "But that's not Stefan's surprise." The excited giddiness in Callie's voice, along with the glow Stef was just noticing on her face, told her everything she needed to know.

"Oh my goodness." Stef clapped her hands over her mouth. "You're pregnant."

Callie's head bobbed with her vigorous nod.

"Oh my *God*. I knew it! I knew it wouldn't be long before you two got pregnant." She wrapped her arms around her sister-in-law, pulling her in for a hug that lasted no less than a full minute. Her arms still clamped on Callie's shoulders, Stef leaned back and looked over her face. It positively beamed. "Stefan is going to be scared shitless. You know that, right?"

"Yes, I know." Callie laughed.

"How far along are you?"

"Three months. I didn't even recognize what was happening until we got home from Grand Turk. I'd skipped a few months, but I've been so nervous about the wedding that I thought it was just the stress. But when I told Kiera and Jada, they immediately demanded I take a pregnancy test."

"Have you only taken the home test?" Stef asked, knowing those were not one hundred percent reliable.

"I went to my doctor yesterday. I'm definitely pregnant."

"Yes! I am so happy for the two of you I can hardly stand it." Stef wrapped her arms around her again. This woman was going to make her knuckleheaded brother a father.

"So, about the surprise," Callie said.

"What do you need me to do?"

"I'm creating a family album, and I need pictures of Stefan as a kid."

Stef grimaced.

"I know," Callie said. "Stefan has told me all about his childhood and his relationship with his dad. From what he's told me, it was pretty rough."

"There are rigid, unfeeling people in this world," Stef said. "My dad happens to be one of them. Stefan and I dealt with it in different ways. Stefan confronted him every chance he could. I rebelled."

And had to count on her dad to bail her out of trouble when her rebelling finally caught up with her.

"Are there *any* happy pictures of Stefan as a child?" Callie asked. "I want to present it to him as sort of a 'starting our lives together' album, with pictures of both of us through the years, then shots from the wedding. At the very end, I'll have a blank birth announcement. Does that sound cheesy?"

"That sounds adorable," Stef said. "But, then again, I love cheesy, so I'm probably not the best person to give advice on it." She waved her hands. "I'll find some pictures. I'm sure my mom has some." She shook her head. "Stefan is going to be ecstatic. After he throws up a few times, of course."

Callie laughed again, but then she sobered, her expression taking on a more somber, cautious look.

"Are you...uh...are you doing okay today?" she asked. Her shoulder lifted in a hesitant shrug. "Before he left the house this morning, Stefan mentioned that today is the anniversary of the accident. At first I assumed he was talking about your late husband, but—"

"No," Stef interrupted. "He's talking about another accident. But, not too worry, I'm doing fine."

"Are you sure? I know it never gets easier,"

Callie said.

Yes, she knew. Her sister-in-law had lost her parents in a car accident back when she was in college. Callie understood grief.

"I'm okay," Stef said. "I promise."

"Well, Stefan will probably call later to check up on you anyway."

"Don't worry, I'll make sure to keep my lips zipped when it comes to the surprise," Stef reassured her.

She promised Callie she'd have some pictures for her by the next afternoon, then actually said a brief prayer of thanks when their conversation was interrupted by EMS's arrival. Thank goodness the patient they'd brought in from the nursing home only had a stomach bug. Stef would have felt really guilty over her relief if it had been something life threatening.

By the time her half-shift ended, she'd managed to quell the disquiet that lingered in her belly from the day's earlier reminders about the accident. As she made her way to her car, her cellphone rang. Stef smiled at the sight of Dustin's name. It was both surprising and a bit alarming. This was supposed to be a temporary friendship. She shouldn't allow just the sight of his name to stir up such excitement within her.

She tried to maintain an air of detachment as she answered, but within seconds his voice drew a smile across her face.

"You're not bailing on me are you?" Dustin

asked.

"No, I'm leaving work right now. Give me about an hour."

"Are you sure you don't want me to come and pick you up?" Dustin asked. "I promise to come in a car this time."

"Dustin, you live in New Orleans. It doesn't make sense for you to drive all the way to Maplesville to pick me up and then have to drive all the way back to bring me home. I can meet you. Of course, it would be nice to know exactly where we're going once I get there."

"You'll find out soon enough." Amusement colored his voice. "Just park in the lot at the base of the French Quarter, the one not far from Decatur Street. I'll see you there."

"Fine," Stef said with a dramatic sigh.

"And get ready to get over that fear of bugs."

Anxiety skated down her spine just at the thought.

Even though ninety percent of her common sense told her to back out of whatever crazy scheme Dustin had prepared for her, she tamped it down and decided to pay attention to the ten percent that was too curious to say no. She wasn't sure why she trusted him, but she did.

"You'll probably regret this," Stef muttered once she got behind the wheel and started en route to New Orleans. She continued to question the wisdom of what she was doing as she traveled south across the yawning stretch of Lake Ponchartrain and into the heart of the French Quarter. Her worry had less to do with whatever bug-related adventure Dustin had up his sleeve; it was more about the man himself. He stirred things within her, feelings that could become addicting if she were not careful. Stef knew it would be dangerous to crave him more than she already did.

She turned into the open-air parking lot that butted against the levee lining the great Mississippi River and found a spot that faced the Beinville streetcar station. As she got out, planning to call Dustin, a gleaming black motorcycle pulled into the empty space alongside her. Its driver straddled his feet on either side and set the kickstand in place. When he took off his helmet, her insides went liquid.

Good Lord, but this man was trying to kill her.

Stef leaned against her driver's side door and folded her arms across her chest. She waited until he'd stowed the helmet in a compartment at the rear of the bike before nodding in the direction of the gleaming machine. "Were you planning to pick me up on this?"

He shook his head. "I was going to use a car, but I can take you for a ride if you want one."

She *so* wanted a ride on his bike. Among other things.

Heat instantly shot down her spine at the

barrage of images flashing across her mind.

The bad girl that lived within her—that crazy, risk-taking adrenalin junky she'd worked so hard to suppress—screamed at her to say yes.

Instead, Stef shook her head. "No thanks."

The temptation was just too great. It would start with a motorcycle ride. Next thing she knew she would be sitting in a jail cell, waiting for her father to bail her out.

Okay, so maybe that was a bit of a stretch, but Stef knew just how quickly things could get out of control. She'd lived it.

"Let me guess," Dustin said, his tone teasing. "The nurse has seen her share of motorcycle crash victims in the ER."

That had nothing to do with her decision not to climb onto that gleaming mass of shiny metal, but it was easier than sharing the harsh truth.

"You got it," she said. Needing a subject change, she asked, "Now, what exactly is there in the French Quarter that can help me get past my bug phobia?"

"You still haven't figured it out?"

She shook her head. Nervousness slid down her spine at the mischievous gleam in his eyes. He rubbed his hands together. "This is going to be fun."

Oh, yeah. She was definitely nervous now.

"By the way, sorry I was a little late."

"You got here a minute after I did," Stef said.

"But I wanted to get here *before* you did. I had to stop in on one of my mechanics. He's been out for a couple of weeks, dealing with an old injury and VA bureaucracy. I went over to his place in Broadmoor to see if I could help him figure it all out."

She looked over at him, staggered by his nonchalance. "You do realize how amazing that is, don't you?" she asked.

"What?"

He truly didn't see it. She was stunned. And, yeah, maybe her heart took a slight tumble for him, too. It was hard not to fall for a combination of gorgeous, hot, funny *and* humble.

"Just a little FYI…most company owners don't make house calls to their sick employees. In fact, most company owners would be trying to find a replacement, not seeing how they can help."

He shrugged. "I came out of Afghanistan in pretty good shape. A few nicks and scratches, but nothing to get too worked up about." He brushed a thumb back and forth along his hip. "Doesn't matter whether you want to call it lucky, blessed, always avoiding the wrong place at the right time—I got out practically unscathed. But we both know our share of men and women who didn't."

Stef nodded. Even without taking into account the injury that had ended her brother's navy career, as an army nurse, she'd treated more than her share of soldiers who had returned home both with physical and mental wounds.

"It's everyone's duty to take care of the vets with battle scars," Dustin continued. "The injuries you can see and those you can't." He tapped the side of his head. "Your brother is the perfect example. Looking at Stefan on the outside, you would never think he suffered an injury severe enough to get him discharged from the navy."

"Stefan is the perfect example of how important what you're doing is to your employees," Stef said. "I don't know what he would have done if not for you. What would *any* of your employees do without you?"

A shadow crossed his face, but before she could question it, he said, "Here we are."

They stood on the sidewalk in front of the stately US Custom House on Canal Street, just before the entrance to the Audubon Institute's Insectarium and Butterfly Garden.

Stef shook her head. "No way."

"What?" Dustin asked. "This is perfect. The best way to get over a fear is to face it head on. You'll be surrounded by thousands of bugs in a controlled environment."

"I run out of the room when commercials for this place come on TV."

"How did you deal with the spiders and

scorpions in Afghanistan?"

"My unit understood my fear. They kept them away from me."

"Wow. That's how they roll in the army? Be happy you weren't with the guys I had to deal with over there. They would have had the entire unit collecting bugs to torture you with."

"Uh, duh. Didn't I tell you what Stefan did to me as a kid? I see now that he fit right in with you crazy navy men." He tugged her by the hand, but Stef refused to budge. "Do I have to?"

"No, but just think of how proud Jacob will be when the two of you are catching lightning bugs?"

"That's a low blow. Mentioning my baby's name at a time like this."

"Whatever it takes," Dustin laughed. "Now, let's go touch some bugs."

"You didn't say anything about touching."

Dustin's shoulders dropped in exasperation. "We'll see how it goes. If you're not ready to touch, then we won't touch." A grin curled the corner of his mouth. "Just to be clear, we're talking about bugs here. When it comes to other things, I definitely want you to touch. I'm *begging* for you to touch."

She cursed every one of the sensual little pinpricks that skidded along her skin. This was *not* the time. In an effort to prevent herself from dragging him to her car and having her way with him in the back seat, Stef took him by the hand and entered the Insectarium.

Dustin claimed they would start out slowly. Apparently, he thought tackling the butterfly garden first would ease her in to seeing the really creepy bugs.

"I'm afraid of butterflies too," she admitted.

"Who in their right mind is afraid of a butterfly?" Dustin asked. His look of incredulousness would have made her laugh if she wasn't scared to death. "What can a pretty insect with wings do to you?"

"I never said my fear was rational," Stef argued.

He dragged her to the exhibit room where hundreds of butterflies flitted around. Her heart beat so fast she could feel it pumping in her ears.

"You really are scared," he said. "Your hands are cold."

"I know. It's ridiculous."

After a significant pause, he said, "No it isn't. We all have something we fear." Another beat passed. "Doesn't matter how outlandish it seems. If you're afraid, then it is what it is."

The seriousness in his voice gave her pause. For a moment, Stef forgot that she was terrified. She was more interested in finding out the story behind his statement than worrying about the swarm of demon insects flittering around her.

"What do you fear?" she asked.

"That I'll never get to see you in that red string bikini."

She elbowed him in the side. "That bikini is a figment of your imagination, remember?"

"I can buy you one." The boyish hope in his eyes drew a sharp laugh from her. "Really," he said. "We can stop over at the Shops at Canal Place when we leave here."

"You're not getting me in a bikini. Just put that dream out of your head."

He snorted. "Army women."

Stef didn't miss that he'd avoided answering her question, but she let it slide for the moment. They still had two weeks together—plenty of time to figure out what that was all about.

After several failed attempts, including a choked scream that turned the heads of other patrons strolling around the butterfly garden, Stef let a small butterfly rest on her hand. She was scared out of her mind, but at least she'd taken this one tiny step.

As they traveled from exhibit to exhibit, her comfort level marginally increased. Stef felt she deserved a medal for getting through the Termite Gallery without scratching her skin off. She hated every second, but at least she wasn't on the verge of bolting anymore. Maybe there was something to Dustin's plan. Eventually, with lots of prayer and screaming, she just might be able to catch fireflies with Jacob.

"There is one more place we have to visit before we leave," Dustin said as they exited the Termite Gallery. He took her by the hand and walked across the corridor.

Stef's feet halted just inside the entryway. "No way. Forget it."

"What? The Bug Buffet is the best part of the Insectarium," he said. "Some of these bugs are delicacies in other parts of the world."

"I am *not* eating a bug."

"What if I dare you?"

Stef shook her head. "I don't care. I'm not doing it."

He crossed his arms over his chest, an inquisitive hitch to his brow. "So, what happens if I dare you to do something and you don't do it? Is it like truth or dare? You have to tell me something that I really want to know? Do something outrageous?"

"Who says I have to do anything? I can just say no and that be the end of it. Period."

"What's the fun in that?"

"I'm not doing it," she repeated.

He put both hands up. "Okay, okay. How about this? I dare you to watch *me* eat something from the bug buffet."

Stef folded her hands over her stomach, but she knew that queasy feeling wasn't going away. "You are a twisted soul, Dustin Patrick." She forced herself to swallow past the revulsion climbing up her throat, but then finally relented. "Fine. But you'd better chew with your mouth closed."

Disgust twisted her lips as they ventured

further into the room. It was filled with kids laughing and joking as they chomped on bugs. Dustin found them a table in the far corner where Stef could look at the wall instead of the bugs being consumed. He left her there for several minutes before returning with a plate.

Stef looked over and spotted two cookies with something that looked like spiders in them. She covered her mouth with her hand and had to force herself not to bolt for the bathroom.

"Why are you groaning? I'm the one who's about to eat it," Dustin said.

She groaned again.

"Bugs have protein." He picked up a cookie. Stef averted her gaze. "No, no, no," he said, capturing her chin and turning her face toward him. "The dare is that you have to watch me while I eat it."

She'd already backed out of one dare. It wasn't as if she faced them often; she couldn't back out of another dare so soon.

The smile on his face was a mile wide as he opened his mouth and took a huge bite out of the cookie.

"Ugh," Stef said, covering her eyes. "That is so gross."

"It's a bit crunchy."

"Stop," she said with a laugh. "You are *so* twisted."

"Can't argue with you there. I've always been a little weird. It's what makes me who I am.

I would have loved coming here when I was a kid."

"So you've always been a daredevil?" she asked.

He took another bite of the cookie then set it back on the tray and dusted off his fingers. Stef tried not to lose the lunch she'd eaten earlier in the hospital cafeteria.

"Actually, I was a runt. A rather timid runt at that," he said. "The daredevil didn't come until much later."

"A runt?" Her eyes traveled down his perfectly chiseled arms and chest. "I find that very hard to believe."

"I'm serious," he said. "You said Jacob is seven, right?" She nodded. "At that age, I was about forty pounds soaking wet and scared of my own shadow. My two older brothers thought I made a better punching bag than a little brother."

Stef instantly sobered. "They hit you?"

"Not enough to leave bruises. It was more roughhousing than being malicious, but I was small, so it hurt a lot more than I let on."

"And your parents didn't say anything?"

"Nah. Both Sidney and Sean were pretty slick when it came to flying under my parents' radar. And they also led me to believe that being a snitch was an offense punishable by death."

"Sidney and Sean? Are they twins?"

He shook his head. "My mom is a big movie

buff. She named us boys after her favorite actors. Dustin Hoffmann, Sidney Poitier, and Sean—"

"Connery." Stef smiled. "That would explain why you think Pierce Bronson was the better 007."

"You got it."

"She really named you all after her favorite actors? That's adorable."

"That's setting your kids up to be teased in school," he said. "Ironically, my two older brothers protected me from bullies. They used to get their kicks out of beating the shit out of me at home, but if anyone dared to touch me at school they'd feel the wrath of the Patrick brothers. Nobody wanted that."

"You're still the younger brother. Do they still try to shove you around?"

"Hell no." Dustin laughed as he shook his head and leaned his chair back on its two hind legs. "I could kick both their asses now. In fact, the first day I arrived back home after basic training, I threatened to give them both a taste of their own medicine. They pretended they didn't know what I was talking about when I told them they deserved some payback for all the whippings I got."

"Are there hard feelings between you guys?"

He shrugged. "I love them, but it's...I don't know...complicated."

"I know a thing or two about complicated

family relationships."

"Yeah, Stefan has told me stories about growing up with your dad. He was never physical, was he?"

Stef shook her head. "No, but sometimes a blistering look from the Lieutenant Colonel could feel like a slap."

"I definitely felt Sean and Sidney's slaps; their taunts, too. In a way, I owe them a lot. They're the ones who put this giant chip on my shoulder. It pushed me to become stronger, work harder. For a long time the driving force behind everything I did, both in the navy and with Hawk Transpo, was to show my brothers what this scrawny kid could do. I love seeing them eat crow."

"I'm guessing they're eating a lot of it these days," she said. "Based on what Stefan has told me about Hawk Transpo, you've built one of the fastest-growing transportation companies the oil and gas industry has ever seen. Your brothers have to respect all you've accomplished."

"They're reluctant to admit it, but I know they do."

He reached for the cookie again. Stef caught his wrist. "Please do not take another bite."

"You want it?"

"No!"

"Come on," he said. "I dare you to take just one bite. You may like the way it tastes."

"I'm okay with never knowing," she said.

110

A slow smile traveled across his lips. "There's another way for you to see how it tastes."

Stef's brow creased, but then understanding dawned. He didn't have to voice his dare for her to know his intentions. And even though a part of her told her to lean back as he leaned forward, a stronger part compelled her to meld her lips against his.

All thoughts of what he'd done with that mouth just a few minutes ago fled as she willingly sank into his slow, deep kiss. His warmth, his flavor, his incredible sensuality — they stole her ability to concentrate on anything but the intoxicating feelings rioting through her blood. With breathtaking slowness he eased his tongue into her mouth.

Something wickedly delicious started to build within Stef's belly. It was slow at first, but the erotic sensations multiplied with every decadent swipe of his tongue.

Her head swam, awareness storming through her. The only coherent thought to make it through the sensual haze clouding her brain was an insistence to give in to this craving that had her on the verge of exploding every time he touched her. He was like a drug. Addictive. Hypnotic.

And she wanted him. All of him.

The reluctance in his groan when he finally pulled away echoed in her own head. With every taste she only craved him more.

"I love that you can't back down from a dare," Dustin said against her lips before finally releasing them.

She couldn't help but laugh at his cockiness. "I've backed down from several dares already," she reminded him.

"Yeah, but I've figured you out. You don't back down from the dares you really want to do." His voice dipped to a low, sexy-as-hell level. "And even though you're fighting it, I know what you really want to do."

A delicious shiver quaked through her. "You're trouble, Dustin Patrick."

He closed in on her lips again, causing tiny pricks of desire to shoot down her spine with his approach.

"Just remember," he whispered against her lips. "A bit of trouble does the body good every now and then."

This time his kiss wasn't as fiery, but it still had Stef on the verge of spontaneously combusting.

Why did she crave him so damn much? Was it because she'd gone so long without feeling desired? Or was it because Dustin harkened to her inner wild child, that rebel who hungered for a taste of adventure? That girl who'd been the cause of so much pain on this very day twelve years ago.

Reality crashed over Stef like a bucket of icy

water.

She pulled away from Dustin's kiss. "We can't do this here," she said, glad for the easy excuse. She glanced over her shoulder and discovered that they were in fact the targets of several less-than-happy stares. "If I brought Jacob here and saw a couple acting the way we are, I would throw a fit."

"Maybe we should get out of here before they call security on us," Dustin said. "Anyway, I'm getting hungry. The cookies were pretty good. But I can use some real food. How about you?"

Stef had only one request. "As long as it's insect free."

He begged Stefanie to let him take her to one of the many fabulous restaurants in the French Quarter, but of all the places she could eat, she wanted a hotdog from a street vendor.

"You're going to love them. I promise," she said when Dustin protested. "These are legendary."

"It's a hotdog. How legendary can it be?"

She shook her head. "It's a Lucky Dog. There's a difference."

If the long line for the hotdog vendor was any indication, maybe there *was* something to her choice. Once they got their food, they climbed a set of stone steps, past several street performers, to a small square across from St. Louis Cathedral. It held a large cannon with Washington Artillery Park etched into its base.

"You think Jacob would like to visit this?" Dustin asked.

"Oh, he'd love it, but I don't have enough room in my house for a diorama of the French Quarter."

He grinned. "Good point."

They strolled across the park to the levee, where they found an empty bench facing the river.

After his first bite Dustin regretted buying only one hotdog. He quickly devoured his and tried not to covet Stefanie's. She was killing him with her dainty little bites.

"You're not getting my hotdog," she said.

Dustin's head flew back with his laugh. "Should I be freaked out that you can read my mind?"

"I don't have to read your mind when you're salivating." She took another bite, then handed him the last piece.

"You're giving me the last of your hotdog? You do realize that's like a declaration of love in my book, right?"

Her laugh made her entire face light up. She might not be ready to declare anything, but he was falling hard.

The lack of panic he felt at the thought

should have shocked him, but instead Dustin embraced it. His laid-back, carefree lifestyle had been the envy of many of his male friends for a long time, but lately *he* was the one who'd found himself fighting waves of jealousy as more and more of his buddies found love. He wanted that bliss he saw on their faces for himself.

"I just remembered...I forgot to mention the party I'm hosting at my place for Stefan and Callie weekend after next."

"I was wondering if you were going to say anything about your little party," she said.

"How do you already know about the party? I only came up with the idea last night." He sat up straight. "Wait. You're not really a mind reader, are you?"

"Callie stopped in to see me at the hospital earlier today," she said. "It took you long enough to mention it. I was starting to think I wasn't invited."

"Not invited? I'm hoping you'll help me plan it. It won't be anything too big. Just a get-together so that Hawk Transpo can all celebrate with them. You up to playing party planner?"

"Of course," she said. "I'd love to help you. Now, you do realize that most bosses don't throw parties for the whole staff when there's an employee wedding, right? This goes above and beyond what typical employers do. These days, most people are happy if there's a potluck dinner at Christmas."

"Stefan deserves it. He works hard. Everyone at Hawk Transpo works hard. The company wouldn't be as successful as it is without the team that works there."

"You built the team. Take some credit here, Dustin."

He shrugged. "I was lucky. I made some really good investments early on, which gave me the capital I needed to get started, but it's been a team effort."

"The humble act is pretty sexy, but I'm not buying it. Luck can only take you so far. It's more than luck. You have to be a savvy businessman and damn smart to accomplish what you have in such a short amount of time."

Dustin rubbed his hands along his thighs before clamping them together. He rested his elbows on his knees.

"I don't share this with everyone," he started. "But I'm kind of a genius."

"You're *kind of* a genius?"

"You know, Mensa member, IQ nearing one-seventy."

"Are you serious?" Incredulousness dripped from her voice.

"I was talking at five months. Started reading when I was two. That's another reason Sid and Sean used to beat me up. Mr. Smarty Pants here garnered a lot of attention as a kid."

"You've got an IQ of 170 and you decided to join the navy? You should be in an office somewhere making millions."

"I am making millions." Dustin chuckled. "That's the coolest thing about my job. I get to make millions and do what I love." He sobered. "Well, at least I *used* to."

She cocked her head to the side. "What do you mean? You don't enjoy your work?"

With another shrug he sat back on the bench, stretching his arms along the back. His hand automatically cupped her shoulder, and she snuggled closer.

"I enjoyed it better when I was actually flying. I don't get up in the air all that much anymore." He looked over at her and grinned. "Except when I'm flying you around so that you can break the law, that is."

She pinched his arm.

"I would have thought you'd be okay working behind the scenes," Stef said. "You've got pilots to do the flying for you. Someone has to run the business."

"Yeah, I know. But it's the flying that got me into this in the first place."

He exhaled a deep breath and dropped his head back. Thick, marshmallow clouds glided across the powder-blue sky, the occasional long-winged crane slicing through it.

"When I was a little boy, I would spend hours stretched out on the grass, looking up at all the planes in the sky. I'd count them as they flew overhead, picturing myself at the controls.

Every year my dad would take us to Colorado Springs for the airshow at the Air Force Academy."

"I'm surprised you didn't join the Air Force, being so close to the academy."

He shook his head. "It wasn't far enough."

"Stefan felt the same way about our dad." She put her hand on his chest, her voice filled with sympathetic understanding. "Your brothers really gave you a hard time, didn't they?"

"They thought they were making me tough." Dustin waved off her concern. "I'm over it. And, in the end, I got the last laugh. You have no idea how much I rub it in their faces when they have to come looking for a loan. I'm not gracious at all. I make their asses grovel."

"It sounds as if they deserve it."

She scooted closer to him; the length of her thigh now touched the entire length of his. Dustin closed his eyes, reveling in the sensation. When he felt her head against his chest his body nearly went up in flames.

He had an hour—possibly two—until he gave up all pretense of being in control, dropped to his knees, and begged her to go to bed with him.

"I can't imagine Stefan and I not getting along," Stefanie said, apparently oblivious to the sensual storm raging inside of him.

Dustin focused his attention on the colorful barges drifting along the river in an attempt to bank that rapidly building fire.

"Stefan was my saving grace in the navy," he said. "We became like brothers."

"You helped him far more than you give yourself credit for." She tilted her head up, her eyes filled with gratitude. "My brother was in a dark place when he was told that he would be medically discharged from the navy. I have no doubt finding Callie is what truly saved him, but that flight instructor job gave him purpose. From what Stefan tells me, you've done the same for quite a few of Hawk Transpo's employees. That's why they're so lucky to have you."

Dustin groaned and ran a hand down his face. "Please, just stop saying that."

Stefanie's head popped up. "What did I say?"

He decided to tell her despite the trepidation clawing at his throat.

"There's this company, Global Offshore Drilling. They have several rigs in the Gulf of Mexico and off the coast of California. A few in Bahrain too, if I'm not mistaken. They've been sniffing around Hawk Transpo for a while now. They want to buy me out."

"Wow," she said, sitting up and turning to face him. "That sounds serious. I'm nosy by nature, so I have to ask —"

"Eighty million," Dustin said.

"Eighty million dollars! I didn't realize your company was worth *that* much."

"It's valued at just under sixty-three million, but based on the trajectory, it'll be worth eighty million within the next few years. Global Offshore is looking to expand their business and Hawk Transpo is just small enough for them to swallow. I've laid the groundwork. I guess they figure it's worth the extra so that they don't have to reinvent the wheel."

"So what are you waiting for to sign on the dotted line? How often is a company willing to buy another company for even more than it's worth? This seems like a no-brainer. You'd never have to work again."

"It's not that simple," Dustin said. "At least not for me. I'm not so sure another company—a company like Global Offshore—would have given Stefan a chance. I knew his work ethic. I knew he was a kickass pilot because I flew alongside him. And I knew he could get the job done, even though others may have given up on him.

"It's the same for most of the people on my payroll. I make it a priority to employ veterans—people who other companies would pass over."

"And you're afraid if you sold the business that the buyer wouldn't make it their priority to continue the tradition."

"Bingo," Dustin said. "Retiring at thirty-five with millions in the bank is more than most people ever dream of, but it's not enough for me. I need to make sure my employees are taken care of."

"My goodness," she said in an awe-filled breath. She placed her hand on his cheek. "Do you realize how amazingly unselfish you are?"

Dustin moved her hand to his lips and kissed the inside of her warm palm. "Don't nominate me for sainthood yet. I haven't turned down the offer."

"The fact that you didn't run straight to that company's headquarters to sign the papers the minute they said eighty million dollars puts you in the saint category. What has to happen for you to make the decision?"

"I'm still not sure," he said.

"Have you talked to your employees?"

He shook his head.

"From everything Stefan has told me, Hawk Transpo is like a family." She ran her hand along his forearm. "You should ask the people you trust the most what they think. Like Stefan. Talk over your options with him, let him be your sounding board." She turned his face toward her again. "Or, if you don't want to ask Stefan, you can ask me."

Dustin's mouth edged up in a small smile. "What do you know about offshore drilling companies?"

"Not a single thing," she said, returning his grin. "But I'm willing to listen if that's what you need."

"There is something you can do for me,"

Dustin said. He pushed back a strand of hair that had escaped her ponytail. "You can tell me why this has to end once Jacob gets back."

She dropped her hand and turned her gaze to the river, but she wasn't getting off that easy. If she was so adamant that their time together be limited to just two more weeks, then she would have to tell him why.

"I'm serious, Stefanie. I want to know why you won't give this a chance. We're just getting started, and we have so much damn fun together. Why end it?"

"Because life isn't all fun and games, Dustin."

"You don't have to tell me that. I've got enough pressure on me to sink a submarine, but I also know that it's important to enjoy myself. Too much of either can be catastrophic. You need to learn how to have a healthy balance."

He waited until she looked at him before he continued with his plea.

"I like you, Stefanie. It scares me how much I like you, but I can't deny what's happening here." He rubbed his flattened palm over his chest. "From that very first night, I liked you enough to risk fighting my best friend if he decided to be an asshole over the two of us seeing each other."

A subtle smile drifted across her lips. "Stefan wouldn't have fought you."

"Only because being with Callie has

mellowed him out. But even if he was still that hothead he'd been back when I first met him—and make no mistake, *that* Stefan would have tried to kick my ass—it didn't matter. What mattered is that I met someone who makes me smile when she smiles. And who likes eating just the white stuff from Oreos, even though it's the most fattening part. And who drives around looking for mud puddles to splash in on a dune buggy ride instead of trying to avoid them.

"We click, Stef. In a way that I've never clicked with someone before. Please don't make me give you up."

"Goodness, Dustin. Stop making this so difficult for me. Please, just stop."

His head fell back as he let out a frustrated sigh. When she pushed up from the bench and walked a couple of yards along the levee, he hesitated then followed her. Taking her shoulders in his hands, he gave them a light squeeze.

"I just want a reason," he said quietly. "Don't I at least deserve a reason? Is it that you're just not feeling me the way I'm feeling you, or what?"

She looked over her shoulder, and the sadness he saw in her eyes crushed him.

"I have my reasons," she said. "But I can't handle talking about them today. Of all days, just not...not today."

She disengaged from his hold and started

left along the levee's paved pathway, toward the parking lot. Dustin rubbed the center of his chest again, trying to get rid of the hollow feeling inside.

Chapter Five

Dustin walked around the rear of the Sikorsky S76 C, inspecting the rear rotor and then running his hand along the tail boom. It was one of more than a dozen in Hawk Transpo's fleet. It still amazed him to think that just a few years ago he'd popped open a bottle of champagne after buying his very first one. Now, he was barreling quickly toward the moment when he would need to make a decision about whether he would sell them all, along with everything else he'd built from the ground up, to Global Offshore Drilling.

"Hawk?"

He turned and spotted Stefan walking toward him, his footsteps echoing on the floor of the vast warehouse.

"What are you doing in here?" his buddy asked.

"You've got a training run scheduled today, don't you?" Dustin asked him. "I'm just checking out everything, making sure it's ready to fly."

"Why are you wasting your time running an inspection? You pay people to do that for you."

"I can look at my own damn helicopter if I want to."

Shit. Way to ensure that Stefan climbed all up in his business.

His friend did not disappoint. Stefan crossed his arms over his chest and tilted his head to the side. "You may want to loosen the elastic in your pantyhose if they're irritating your ass this much."

"Dammit." Dustin ran a hand down his face.

"What's going on?" Stefan asked. When Dustin didn't answer right away, Stefan pressed on. "Hawk?"

"I miss this part, okay." He shook his head, huffing out a humorless laugh. "I miss it. When I started this company, I had one helo and one pilot. Me. Now, just look at this." He flung his arms out to encompass the warehouse. There were nearly two dozen helicopters with the capability of flying out over two hundred oilrig workers at one time.

"Do you realize what you have here?" Stefan asked him. "Do you understand what you've built in this short amount of time, and how fucking amazing it is?"

"Yeah, but amazing for who. I don't get to actually *do* any of it anymore. Hell, I don't have enough hours behind the controls of a dual-engine to fly it if I wanted to."

"Then go and get your hours. What in the hell is stopping you?"

"You don't get it."

"Yes, I do," Stefan said. "If anyone knows

what it means to miss flying, I'm your guy."

Dammit. Now he felt like an asshole.

At least he *could* fly if he wanted to. With Stefan's eye injury, he would never wrap his hands around the controls of a helicopter and take flight again.

"You miss being in the air?" Stefan continued, his voice taking on that taunting quality that used to irritate the hell out of Dustin when they were in the navy. "You want to take the new guy up in the helo today? Go for it," Stefan said. "I'll go in your office, put my feet up on your desk and take a nice, long nap."

"You gonna negotiate the contracts that are on the desk, as well?" Dustin asked. "How about the new safety regulations that just came down from the FAA? The stack is about an inch thick. You want to read through those? Because if you're going to sit at my desk, you'll need to do all the shit that I have to do."

"Spare me this whiny crap," Stefan said. "You don't have to do it all. You can hire someone to take over all of that in the same way you hired me to teach because you were tired of doing it." Stefan folded his arms over his chest. "Now tell me what's really going on here, Hawk?"

Tell him.

The voice in his head was both loud and forceful, but Dustin managed to tamp it down. He knew Stefan had a point. His company had grown so quickly that he had yet to adjust to the idea that he didn't have to do it all.

If he sold to Global, he wouldn't have to do any of it. That carefree life was within his reach. Why was it so damn hard to make a decision?

"Don't pay me any attention," Dustin said. "I'm just in a bad mood."

Stefan's eyes narrowed further. "Did you get in a fight with my sister?"

"No," Dustin said. "Your sister…" He shook his head.

"What about my sister?"

"Your sister confuses the hell out of me." Once he started going, Dustin couldn't stop. "Everything has been great. Better than great. It's been amazing. I've gone to Maplesville every evening for the past week and a half and every day has been more amazing than the last. We've worked on Jacob's diorama together; we've gone looking for lightening bugs. I even hired Kiera Coleman to cater this romantic dinner for us with candles and wine — the whole nine yards."

Even though there was no one else around to hear them, Dustin lowered his voice when he said, "Last night, when we played Scrabble, I could have made *quartz* on a triple word score, but I made *art* instead. I've never liked a woman enough to pass on a seventy-two-point word for her." He ran his hands down his face. "I haven't felt this way about anyone in so long—if ever. But it hasn't been enough. She's still holding back from me and insisting that we end this. I don't understand why she doesn't open up to me."

Stefan put both hands up. "Are we really having this conversation? No, really?" He looked around. "There are hidden cameras, right? You're putting this up on YouTube."

"Can you be serious?"

"Not when you're talking to me like we're starring in a movie on the Lifetime Network."

"Dammit, Stefan, help me out."

"Why would I help you get closer to my sister when I'm not even sure I *want* you to get closer to her?"

Dustin looked him dead in the eye. "You know I'm good for her."

"Shit." Stefan blew out a breath. "I guess if Stef is going to get involved with anyone I'd rather it be someone I trust. Someone who knows that I would kick his ass if he hurt her."

"She's not letting me get close enough to hurt her, not as if I ever would," Dustin said. "She's insisting that we have to stop seeing each other when Jacob gets back from his grandparents this coming Friday, and I don't understand why."

"I seriously cannot believe we're having this conversation."

"Stefan—" Dustin took a step toward him, his hands clenching into fists.

"Calm down." Stefan put both hands up

again. "Look, Stef has been through a lot. It hasn't been all that long since Brandon died. Maybe she's not ready for Jacob to see her dating another man."

"She told me herself that she's at peace with his death."

Stefan hunched his shoulders. "I don't know what you want me to say."

"You're twins. You don't have any kind of weird, psychic twin shit going on between you two?"

Stefan's blank stare only irritated Dustin further.

"Are we finished here?" he asked.

"I guess so," Dustin said. "Seeing as you're not going to help me."

"Actually, I am going to help you. I have the perfect thing to get your mind off both your woman troubles and your helo envy." Stefan clamped a hand over his shoulder and guided him toward the warehouse's double exit doors. "You can go into that cushy ass office and finish planning the fabulous party you're throwing for my beautiful wife and I. Doesn't that sound like fun?"

Dustin cut his eyes at him. "Have you always been this much of an asshole?"

"It takes one to know one, my brother. I think it's why we get along so well."

"Damn, you look hot. You're too far from the camera. Come in closer and turn around so I can see your butt."

"What's the big deal?" Stef said as she twisted her rear end toward the computer screen. "They're just blue jeans."

Tania's loud whistle came through the speakers. "No they are not. Those are peel-off-my-legs-and-do-me jeans."

"That's not a thing."

"Is too."

Stef rolled her eyes. "You may want to tone it down before you have everyone in that coffee shop sneaking peeks at my ass."

"Who cares if they want to see your ass? We should be more concerned with making sure Dustin wants to see it."

"This is *not* a big deal," Stef reiterated. "I'm only going over there to help him lay out the floor plan for Callie and Stefan's party. I've already told him that this...this thing we have going on has to end once Jacob gets back tomorrow."

"I don't understand your reasoning behind that decision either," Tania remarked. "But then again, I'm not a parent. I'll defer to your judgment on this one."

"Believe me, it's for the best."

"So, what's the plan tonight? Are you going to sleep with him? You know farewell sex is the best sex ever."

"Sleeping with him is not on the agenda," Stef said. "Things will be awkward enough when we run into each other from now on. You think knowing that he's seen me naked will help the situation?"

"No, but at least you'll have seen *him* naked too. I think you should go for it," her friend said. "There's no way he's resisting you tonight. I mean, look at you!"

Stef looked down at the light-blue wrap shirt and fitted blue jeans and had to admit that they were not her typical Thursday evening attire. After her shift at the hospital, she'd come home, showered, and tried on four different outfits before finally settling on this one.

"You know how I can tell this is a big deal?" Tania persisted. "You wouldn't have gotten that haircut if it wasn't."

Stef ran her fingers through the thick, chin-length strands. "I got the haircut because I wanted a new look," she said. "It has nothing to do with Dustin."

At least, she hadn't thought it had anything to do with Dustin at the time.

"I call bullshit," Tania said. "The new clothes and new hair has 'come and do me' written all over it, and for you, that's a big deal. I'm starting to believe that you meeting this guy wasn't just a random coincidence. He seems too perfect for you."

"You don't even know him. How can you tell that he's perfect for me?"

"Because even though the camera on this computer isn't worth shit, I can still see how happy you look. I haven't seen you this excited since college."

Stef instantly sobered.

"Dammit, Stefanie." She jumped at the sternness in her friend's voice. "Wipe that frown from your face right this instant," Tania said. "What is it going to take to make you see that I'm happy to see you have fun?"

"I know that," she said.

"Like hell, you do. You can't even allow yourself to smile in front of me. Do you know how that makes me feel?"

Stef's head popped up. She stared at the computer screen, confused. "Why should *you* feel bad? The blame belongs right here." Stef pointed to her chest.

"You've carried it long enough," Tania said. "Don't you think it's past time you forgave yourself for that night?"

She could only stare at her friend's face for a moment before focusing on the framed photo of roasted coffee beans hanging on the wall of whatever coffee shop Tania had dipped into for free wifi.

"I'm working on it," Stef said.

"Work harder. You try to hide it when I'm around, but I can see the guilt you're still carrying. I've missed my old friend who wasn't ashamed to feel happy around me. It's been nice seeing that little glimpse of her lately."

"I promise I'll smile more," Stef said.

"You know what will *really* make you smile? If you get some Flyer Boy nookie tonight."

Stef burst out laughing.

"Oh, crap. I have to go," Tania said. "This place only allows an hour of wifi access at a time and my hour is almost up."

"Take care of yourself out there," Stef said.

"I will. You need to get going. You've got a man who's waiting to ogle your hot ass. Don't keep him waiting."

Stef laughed despite herself. "I'll talk to you later," she said before signing off the web chat. She remained in front of the camera, turning from left to right, studying the snug fit of the form-fitting jeans.

She *was* looking damn good. If she were a guy, she would do herself.

But despite what Tania suggested, Stef knew farewell sex was not in the cards tonight.

After the way things ended last night during their impromptu Scrabble game, Stef wasn't sure Dustin would even want her coming over to his place to help plan the party. Their night had ended in the same way their dates usually ended, with Dustin upset that she wouldn't budge on her stance that all things must come to an end tomorrow. But he had been more upset than usual, which, she guessed, was understandable. The ticking of the clock was getting louder and louder as Jacob's return from Florida drew nearer.

But Stef had started to rethink her all or nothing position. She wanted to end their time together on a more positive note. Tonight, she planned to propose that they remain friends, or at least friendly toward each other. Stef was confident that the man she'd come to know over the past few weeks would go along with that.

She walked over to the mirror and surveyed her new do. Stef still wasn't sure what made her turn into the salon on her way home from work yesterday and demand that the hairdresser cut off eight inches. She figured she would curse the spur-of-the-moment decision the first time she was running late and couldn't put her hair up in a quick ponytail, but for now, she was in love with her new look. She felt sexy. Alive.

So maybe it did have something to do with Dustin. But it was more than just him. She felt like the old Stef.

The thought still terrified her, but not as much as it had just a short time ago. Over the past two weeks she'd discovered that she could let her hair down for a tiny bit without going completely over the edge. She didn't have to go cliff diving, or on month-long motorcycle trips, or any of those other wild and crazy things she used to do. Just a little fun was enough to give her life the spark she needed.

The key element, of course, was Dustin.

He'd helped her to find that part of herself again. His kindness, his carefree spirit, his endearing sense of humor—they all called to that part of her that had been hiding for so long.

So why are you so quick to end it?

"Yes, Stef. Why?" she said aloud.

The more time she spent with him, the flimsier her excuses for why this had to end seemed. There was no good reason for her to stop seeing Dustin. How could she justify it, when the one person who had every right to begrudge Stefanie's happiness encouraged—no, *demanded*—she see this thing through?

Having Tania's blessing only confirmed the instinct Stef had been fighting since the trip to Turks and Caicos. It was all too easy to imagine what a real relationship with Dustin would look like. When she closed her eyes at night, she dreamed of how the upcoming days, months, even years would play out if she just gave him a chance.

Having that effortless smile greet her on a daily basis would be like heaven on earth. Having another man in Jacob's life would be the answer to her prayers.

Dustin wouldn't replace her son's father— no one could or would ever do that—but he would be a wonderful role model for Jacob. His giving heart, his strong work ethic, the empathy he showed to the people who worked for him—they were all the values she wanted to pass on to Jacob.

Why wouldn't she give them a chance?

Stef reached into her jewelry box and grabbed her aquamarine stud earrings. As she brushed her shorter locks to the side, the tiny scar behind her ear that she'd gotten in the accident twelve years ago answered the question for her, reminding her of the danger in embracing this new relationship with Dustin.

Dustin brought out that wild and reckless side in her. It was the side that needed to remain buried.

With a final look in the mirror, Stef wiped the regret from her face and headed out of the house. An hour later, she sat at the curb behind the wheel of her car, convinced that the GPS had guided her to the wrong address.

"Well, he does have millions," Stef reminded herself as she looked up and down tree-lined Prytania Street.

And there was no doubt he'd spent several of them on this house. Buying one of the historic mansions in the heart of New Orleans's Garden District must have set him back a couple of million, at least. But the man traveled by helicopter, why wouldn't he live in a mansion?

Just as she opened her car door, the understated front door of the Italianate-style home opened and Dustin walked out. He hustled down the eight steps two at a time and jogged to the wrought iron gate, opening it for her.

"You cut your hair," he said by way of greeting.

Her hand shot self-consciously to her head. "Uh, yeah. I wanted to try something new."

"I like it. It fits you. Why didn't you call to say you were here?" he asked.

"I wasn't sure I was at the right place," Stef said. "This is...something else. I mean, I knew you had money. I just never pictured you living in a place like this. I thought of you more as a sleek, modern condo kind of guy."

"Yeah, I know it's a bit over-the-top for one person," he said, glancing over his shoulder. "My real estate agent was a smooth talker. He convinced me that I deserved a house of this magnitude. Turns out I only needed a house about a third of this size. Most of the rooms go unused."

His demeanor lifted the slight trepidation she'd felt just before she arrived. After the way things ended between them last night, a tiny part of her feared that he would tell her he no longer needed her help. Blessedly, it seemed as if he was in no hurry to pick up the conversation that had ended with him leaving in the middle of their Scrabble game, disgruntled because she remained steadfast in her insistence that things between them end with Jacob's return.

As if he'd read her mind, he said, "I'm not bringing up last night, Stefanie. I don't want anything to spoil our last day together."

She swallowed deeply and nodded.

"What time does Jacob come home tomorrow? "

"They land just after three in the afternoon. Shelia, his grandmother, is flying him over."

He sucked in a deep breath and slid his hands in his pockets.

"Well, I guess that's that. We can't hang out anymore after today."

"Dustin—"

"I'm respecting your wishes. It's what you want, so it's what it has to be. Let's just enjoy this evening." A roguish grin drew across his lips. "I've got some conch fritters, Bond movies, and grape Kool-Aid waiting for us after we're done planning the party layout."

Stef burst out laughing. Gratefulness for his understanding swelled within her. He had every right to be surly and difficult; instead he wanted to make it easy for her.

Giving him up would be one of the hardest things she ever had to do.

Dustin took her on a tour of the massive house. He was right—this was excessive, especially for a single man. Now, if he had a family...

Stef elbowed that thought out of her head.

The thought of Dustin bringing another

woman into this house, starting a family with her, made Stef want to throw herself over the double staircase's ornate railing. In all of her insistence that their time together be temporary, she had never once considered how much it would hurt when he started dating someone else.

It wasn't realistic to think that she would never see him again. He was Stefan's best friend. Their paths would eventually cross at backyard gatherings, possibly on holidays. How would she stomach the first time she saw another woman on his arm?

The thought twisted her gut, but Stef breathed her way through it. She refused to spend her final evening with Dustin thinking about his future women.

By the time they finished the tour of the house, dusk had fallen, which was perfect since Stefan and Callie's party would take place at night this coming Saturday. She could check out the lighting in his backyard where the party would be held, and figure out if they needed more.

Stefanie released an awed gasp when they stepped out into his backyard. It was breathtaking. A dual Roman-end pool sat as the focal point, with a perfectly manicured hedge garden maze on one side. There were several marble statues peppered throughout the gardens, each lit with its own spotlight.

On the other end of the pool sat a gorgeous open pool house. The two front columns rose out of the edge of the pool. The space was large enough to hold a sofa and two long chaises. A massive stone fireplace was built into the center of the backyard.

"Tell the truth," Stef said, "this is the reason you bought this house. This is gorgeous."

"I probably spend more time out here than I do inside," Dustin admitted.

He pointed to where he envisioned staging different aspects of the party — food, music, gifts, an open bar. He planned to rent sofa and loveseats, along with several fire tables, to make the area more cozy.

"It just seems more intimate than wooden folding chairs. I want people to feel comfortable."

"I think it's a wonderful idea," Stef said. "You don't need my input. You have this under control."

He slid his palms around her hips, resting his hands at the small of her back. "Actually, I hired an event planner to do the heavy lifting. Everything for the party is just about taken care of. Asking you to help was just an excuse to get you here."

"You ever thought about just inviting me?"

He tilted his head to the side, his brow furrowing with his frown. "Why didn't I think of that?"

Her shoulders shook with her soft chuckle. She leaned into him, placing her head on his chest.

"That pool looks incredible," she said.

"You want to go swimming?"

Stef leaned her head back, looking up at him. "I didn't bring a suit."

The grin that curled up the side of his mouth was the epitome of wicked. "You're going to let that stop you?"

Awareness quaked in her belly, even as her skin burned with desire. It was time for her to be honest with herself. She'd wanted this from the moment she met him. The tight jeans, the new haircut; they were not just about her finding her way back to her old self. They were about making Dustin want her as much as she wanted him.

Tonight was their last night together. She would get what she wanted.

Her eyes trained on him, Stef shrugged out of his arms and backed away, slipping out of her sandals and kicking them to the side. She caught the measured rise and fall of Dustin's chest as his gaze followed her hand to the snap on her jeans. She unzipped them, then hooked her thumbs along the waist and pulled them down over her hips.

"Stefanie." Her name exited his mouth on a hoarse whisper.

She gathered the hem of her shirt and pulled

it over her head.

"God. Stefanie," Dustin said, reaching for her. She moved to the side, and put her hand behind her back, fingering the bra clip. She unhooked the single clasp and pulled the bra straps down her arms, releasing the fabric with a flick of her wrist.

Dustin's desperate moan drizzled over her like warm honey. It was all the encouragement she needed to make her final move.

Chapter Six

A pair of white satin panties hit Dustin square in the chest, and just like that, everything in his body went instantly, incredibly hard. He brought the silky fabric to his face and inhaled Stefanie's musky scent, his eyes falling shut as a tidal wave of desire crashed through him. The need to devour her intensified, setting his blood on fire.

Dustin's eyes widened as she dove into the pool, gracefully slicing the surface.

"Am I the only one skinny dipping here?" she called over her shoulder. She kicked her joined feet, splashing at him like a mermaid. The water droplets on her naked skin glistened under the soft lighting illuminating the pool.

He should wait until he was able to bring his body back under control, but as he stared at her naked form gliding through the water, Dustin realized that probably wouldn't happen for the rest of the night.

He made quick work of shucking the clothes from his body, his erection springing from his boxers as he yanked them down his legs.

"Wow," Stefanie said with a low laugh. "Someone's happy."

"Happy? I'm fucking ecstatic."

Dustin dove into the heated water, quickly swimming to where she floated in the center of the pool. He turned her naked body against his and discovered what heaven felt like as they treaded water together. Arms and legs entwined, he swam them toward the pool steps. Once they were at the shallow end, he cornered her against the wall.

He caged her within his arms, his fisted palms on either side of her. Staring into those liquid brown eyes, he leaned forward and joined his mouth with hers. He reveled in the perfection of her lips, trailing his tongue along the seam before thrusting inside. Her exquisite breasts brushed against him. He lifted her higher and dipped his head, capturing one marble-hard nipple between his lips. He toyed with the stiff pebble, lapping his tongue around and around, squeezing it between his lips before sucking it fully inside his mouth.

Her throaty moan compelled him to try other ways to make her duplicate the erotic sound. For this one moment in time, his entire purpose in life centered on giving her as much pleasure as she could possibly stand.

Dustin showed her other breast the same attention he'd lavished on the first. The satisfaction he derived from hearing her husky groans and low, pleasure-soaked whimpers made him dizzy with the knowledge of what was to come.

Stefanie cupped his face in her hands and pulled his lips to hers. She wrapped her legs high around his waist and plunged her tongue into his mouth.

"Damn." The gruff curse tore from his throat. "I would have said to hell with that dune buggy ride back on Grand Turk if I knew skinny dipping in the ocean was an option."

Stefanie released a husky laugh. "Who says I would have gone skinny dipping with you back on Grand Turk? I hardly knew you then."

"You would have if I'd dared," he whispered against her lips.

The sultry heat in her gaze was hot enough to singe his skin. "This time I'm the one making the dare," she said.

"Oh yeah?" Dustin managed to get out past the lust clogging his throat. "What's the dare?"

"I dare you to make me scream from now until morning."

He hooked his arms behind her knees and lifted her out of the water. "You're on."

Carrying her to the pool house, he draped her over one of the chaises. He trailed his fingers along her wet skin, bringing them to her inner thighs and spreading her legs apart. His breath quickened as need hit him hard and fast.

He put his mouth to her glistening center and began to feast on the delectable heaven between her legs.

Nothing in life could have prepared him for that first sensual taste of her. Dustin settled in for the long haul. He lingered between her thighs, varying both his pace and pressure. He teased her delicate flesh, stroking up one side and down the other, then he buried his face against her, drinking in the fragrant dampness that soaked her skin. He swirled his tongue around her pulsing center before flicking it in rapid succession over the tightening bundle of nerves tucked at her clef.

Every mewl of pleasure that escaped her throat heightened the desire coursing through him. It pushed him to lick harder, stroke faster. Dustin closed his mouth over her clit and sucked for all he was worth. He wanted to devour every drop of her flavor.

Stefanie's back bowed. Her thighs tightened around his head as her scream tore through the air. After bringing her to orgasm once more with his mouth, he trailed his tongue up her body, peppering her moist skin with kisses.

"Sit tight for a minute," he whispered into her ear. "I have to go in the house to get a box of condoms."

Her brow arched. "A box?"

"Hell yes. I've been dreaming about this from the minute we first met. I don't plan to finish with you for hours."

The moment Dustin left her Stef braced herself for the rush of conscience that would have her scrambling to put her clothes back on and run out of here, but it never came. She was not running away from this.

Even though she'd told herself that tonight was about them ending their time together as friends, she knew in her heart that this is what she wanted to happen all along. She wanted to feel Dustin's naked body against her own. She wanted—even if just for one night—to share this experience with him.

When Dustin emerged from the house carrying the box of condoms and a bottle of wine, Stef couldn't help but laugh.

"You really brought an entire box of condoms?"

"I warned you," he said. "You're in for a long night."

He set both items on the glass end table, unwrapped one condom and rolled it over his erection. Stef's limbs quivered in anticipation of what would happen next.

Dustin came over to the chaise and covered her body with his. Stef wrapped her arms around his neck. "Now, are you going to take on that dare, or what?" she whispered against his jaw.

He lowered himself between her legs. "You only have to dare me once."

Stef closed her eyes and allowed herself to retreat to the erotic sanctuary Dustin created for her. She journeyed deeper with every delicious slide of his thick erection.

Sensation pulsed within her, bright and searing, the intensity building at a rate that both scared and thrilled her. She tried to control the feelings blossoming in her chest as Dustin penetrated her soul as well as her body, but it was no use. His tender, yet fierce, possession rendered her helpless to fight the love suddenly overwhelming her.

She locked her legs at the small of his back and moved her body with his, rocking into his thrusts, staking claim to every drop of pleasure he sought to give her. She let out a soft cry as he ground his hips against hers, plunging deep, nearly pulling out, and then plunging again.

Wrapping his arms around her, Dustin flipped them over and fitted her on top of his rock hard length. He dug his fingers into her hips and guided her movements, lifting her up, and then tugging her down as his hips rose to meet her.

The puckered skin of a scar on his leg abraded her inner thigh, the friction as erotic and intimate as his gaze on her breasts.

"Faster," he gritted through clenched teeth, his fingers sinking into her ass as he tightened his grip.

Blood pounded through her veins,

thunderous, deafening. Stef braced her hands against his chest, using it for leverage as she rode him hard. The sound of their wet skin slapping together echoed in the dark stillness surrounding them. Passion raged within her, the erotic melody of their lovemaking stoking the fire in her belly, spearing her with quick, sharp stabs of desire.

"*Faster*," Dustin practically roared, flipping her over again and bringing her legs over his shoulders. The angle allowed him to plunge deeper than any man ever had, his thick cock pumping in and out with fluid, rapid thrusts.

In a matter of seconds Stef's world split in two. She rushed headlong into the blinding whirlwind of pleasure. Her entire body shook with it, the powerful force of her orgasm stealing the breath from her lungs.

Dustin continued thrusting. He took both of her hands in his, lacing their fingers together, binding their souls as surely as he bonded their bodies. Pleasure ripped through her a second time, the force of it depleting every ounce of her strength.

Dustin's body shivered above her as he climaxed, the veins in his neck pronounced as they strained against his skin. His body jerked several times before he collapsed on top of her and buried his face against her neck.

Stefanie ran her hands up and down his back, loving the feel of his warm moist skin.

Loving…him.

She fought the realization that was slowly taking shape in her head, but the truth was too powerful to deny. She was falling in love with him.

And after tonight this passion they'd discovered together would come to an end.

Chapter Seven

Stef looked out over the waves slowly rippling along the pool's surface. Lights embedded into its walls gradually changed the water's color from magenta to gold to green to blue.

Dustin had taken a blanket from the storage space discreetly disguised as an ottoman. He'd draped it over them after the second — or was it the third? — time they'd made love.

Stef had no idea what time it was, nor was she in any hurry to find out. Every second that ticked by brought her closer to the time she would have to leave Dustin, and the thought of leaving him hurt too much to think about it.

She buried her head in the bend of his strong arm, cocooning herself in his warmth. She knew Dustin was awake. She could tell by the change in his breathing. It was no longer the deep, steady breaths of sleep, yet he remained silent. It was as if they both were trying to preserve the delicate shelter the last few hours had built around them. As if they both knew that words would shatter it.

"Help me to understand, Stefanie." Dustin's softly spoken words cut through the stillness. He caressed her bare shoulder with gentle strokes, his fingers drawing circles on her skin. "If you still insist that we end this, even after everything tonight, you're going to have to explain why."

He tilted her face toward him. "Is it that you don't think Jacob is ready to see you with another man? If that's the case, he doesn't have to know just yet. We can be discreet."

"I would never hide you from my son," Stef said. "It's not likely I could even if I wanted to. He's very perceptive for his age."

"So, is it you? Are *you* not ready to take this step yet? Is it still too close to your husband's death?"

Stef almost grabbed on to the gift he'd handed her, but guilt wouldn't allow her to do it. She would not besmirch her late husband's spirit by using him as an excuse.

"I loved Brandon," she started. "He was one of the kindest, gentlest souls I've ever known. But over the last couple of years of our marriage, we were more like friends than husband and wife." She felt Dustin's arms stiffen around her. "There was love—there had always been love between us—but there was never real passion. Not even in the beginning."

It pained her to reveal such intimate details about her marriage. Stef had never shared her secret with anyone, not even Tania.

"Why did you marry him?"

"Because Brandon was the kind of man I needed in my life. He kept me grounded, reined me in when I needed it the most." She twisted around so that she could look at him. "Do you want to know why being with you scares me? Because you bring out feelings in me I've tried to suppress for years. You make me want to do the kind of things that led to one of darkest parts of my past. I promised myself that I would never be that girl again."

"But why? What's so wrong with being that girl?" When she didn't answer, he squeezed her shoulders gently but firmly. "Stefanie, talk to me."

"I *can't* be her! Because that girl…" She stopped, sucked in a deep, fortifying breath. "That girl nearly killed her best friend. That girl is the reason my best friend, Tania, has a prosthetic leg."

Dustin stared at her for several heartbeats, saying nothing. When he finally spoke, Stef's heart lurched at the tender understanding in his voice.

"What happened?" he asked.

Her eyes fell shut. It took her a moment before she could bring herself to continue.

"I was in my early twenties, before I joined the army. I was always a bit of a wild child, but once I got to college it got worse."

"Drinking?"

She shook her head. "I never drank. I just don't like the way alcohol tastes."

"Drugs?" he asked

"I didn't need drugs. I got high on adrenalin. One night my best friend and I went club hopping. These guys challenged us to a street race. I wanted to prove how badass I was, so I pushed the car to its limit and it spun out of control. We hit a guardrail."

"Thank God it wasn't a tree or a concrete wall."

"I was lucky." She swallowed audibly, her throat growing drier with each word. "I escaped with a few cuts and bruises and a broken ankle. My best friend, Tania, wasn't so lucky, though. She *was* drunk and hadn't buckled her seatbelt. She went through the windshield. The glass damaged her leg so badly that it had to be amputated just below her knee."

That night had been a turning point—*the* turning point—in her life.

Seeing the disappointment on her father's face when he came to pick her up at the hospital was one of the most devastating experiences she'd ever endured. She still didn't know what kind of strings he'd pulled to keep her out of jail, and she'd never asked. She'd just vowed to never go back to being that girl again.

"And you blame yourself," Dustin stated.

"There's no one else to blame," Stef returned. "My dad, who was respected and well-liked by law enforcement in the area, managed to prevent me from getting arrested. I was cited for reckless driving. That's it. He made me join the army soon after and told me that if I didn't straighten up I could forget about him ever saving my ass again."

"What happened to your friend? Do the two of you still talk, or was that the end of your friendship?"

"She helped me pick out the shirt I wore tonight," Stef said with a sad smile. "She has never blamed me, but that doesn't mean that I'm not the one to blame."

Several charged seconds ticked by before Dustin spoke again. "Stefanie, I'm sorry for what happened to you, and to your friend. But I still don't understand what it has to do with us being together."

Regret thudded against her chest with every heartbeat, but it would pale in comparison to what she would feel if she ever slipped into her old ways again and caused another catastrophe.

"I…" She cleared her throat. "I can't be with you, because you make me feel like that girl I used to be," she said. "You make me crave the adrenalin rush. When I'm with you, I do wild and crazy things, like breaking into the Chalmette Battlefield and skinny-dipping in your backyard, and I *love* it."

She looked him in the eyes.

"Do you understand now, Dustin? I love that feeling. I crave it, like a drug. That's what scares me the most. When I'm with you I want to be that carefree and reckless Stefanie I used to be. And I just can't afford to go down that path again, not when I have Jacob. I have to consider how my actions would affect him."

"You were a young, reckless girl with no responsibilities back then. But you're older and wiser now. There's a difference between being reckless and enjoying the occasional adrenalin rush. You can trust yourself to tell the difference."

"Can I?" She looked out over the pool again and then back up at him. "That's just it, Dustin. I don't know if I can trust myself. It's a slippery slope. It can start with something as innocent as what we've been doing over these past two weeks, then the next thing you know, I'm pressing harder on the pedal on my way from work, trying to see how fast I can push my car." She shook her head. "It's safer if I just stay away from that path altogether. I don't care if it makes me a boring, suburban mom."

"So that's it then," Dustin said. The frustration in his voice tore at Stef's soul. She never meant to hurt him. But, then, he wasn't the only one hurting.

"That's it," she said, placing her head on his broad chest one last time. "I'm sorry it has to be this way, but it does. I have too much to lose."

Stef stood just outside the security

checkpoint of Concourse B at Louis Armstrong International Airport. She stared through the Plexiglas walls, looking for the first sight of her mother-in-law's short, natural afro, or Jacob's head bobbing between the airline passengers making their way to their respective gates.

The moment she spotted them a smile broke out across her face. It was the first time she'd felt anything other than despair since leaving Dustin's home that morning. Jacob came through the gate and ran into her open arms. Stef held him to her chest, kissing the top of his bristly hair. She held onto him for several seconds longer than necessary. She would have to think long and hard before she allowed him to leave for this long again.

She finally released Jacob from the bear hug and walked over to the Plexiglas. Boarding for Shelia's return flight to Tampa would start in just a few minutes. They had already decided that she wouldn't chance going back through the security line.

Stef put her hand up to the glass. "Thank you," she said.

"Thanks for sending him." Her mother-in-law's eyes glistened with tears. "Grandma will miss you," she said to Jacob before blowing him a kiss.

Once Shelia left for her gate, Stef and Jacob headed for baggage claim. Her son insisted that he was strong enough to roll his luggage to the covered parking garage. He fumbled a couple of times trying to get it to stand upright, but once the casters were all pointed in the right direction it was smooth sailing.

Watching his confident stride caused a pinch in Stef's chest. She wasn't ready for this little show of independence just yet, but she knew there was no way to stop it. He was growing up so much quicker than she'd anticipated.

Jacob's initial questions were about Sandy. Even though Stef had held the cat in her arms several times during their web chats so that he could see with his own eyes that his pet was being well taken care of, he still wanted to know how she was doing. He then started in on all the rides he'd been tall enough to ride at the various Florida theme parks. He'd become a bona fide chatterbox.

He stopped to take a breath and Stef saw her opening.

"Hey," she said as she took the on-ramp onto Interstate 10. "I'm off for the rest of the day. I thought we could go to that bouncy house place where Durrell had his birthday party."

"But I'm sleeping over at Andre's tonight," Jacob said from his booster seat in the back.

Stef's eyes flashed to the rearview mirror. "Since when?"

"He asked me last night. Grandma said I could."

"The same Grandma who is on her way to

Florida?" Stef asked. "I thought you were going to a sleepover at Travis's house tomorrow so that I can go to Uncle Stefan and Aunt Callie's party."

"Yep, I'm going to Travis's, too."

Her son, the social butterfly.

Jacob reached over and patted her arm. "Don't worry, Mom. We have time to hang out later once I've seen all my friends."

"Thanks a lot." Stef released a rueful laugh. "It's okay. I'll just have to find some friends of my own."

"You should," Jacob said with a head nod. Then he went back to playing whatever handheld device Shelia and Robert had bought him.

Stef divided her attention between the long stretch of the Causeway Bridge ahead of her and looking at the top of her son's bowed head in the rearview mirror. If she were being honest with herself, she could admit that she had slowly come to realize that she was never in any real danger of slipping back into her old, reckless ways, because she could never do anything that would bring him harm. The little boy whose fingers were flying furiously over the handheld game was her life; he was the reason she even bothered to take a breath. How could she ever think she was capable of putting anything as trivial as an adrenalin rush before him?

Yet, that's why she'd broken things off with

Dustin. She'd turned away the first man to make her feel alive in years, all because she was too afraid he would turn her into something she was never in danger of becoming.

A soft cry escaped her throat at the thought of what she'd given up.

"What's wrong, Mom?"

"Nothing," Stef said quickly. She smiled at him through the rearview mirror. "Nothing's wrong, baby."

It was a lie. Something was definitely wrong. And, once again, it was all her fault.

But this time she would fix it.

Dustin pressed his steepled fingers against his lips as he studied the words he'd just typed in the e-mail. The knot that had been residing in his stomach for the past few months was still there, but had started to loosen the tiniest bit.

He'd decided to take Stefanie's advice and bring his employees—his family—in on the discussion about Global Offshore Drilling. He should have done this a long time ago.

He hit send, mailing the meeting request to the eight men and women who had been employed at Hawk Transpo the longest, along with Stefan, whose opinion Dustin trusted the most out of all of them. He'd instructed them to meet him in the conference room in an hour.

The deadline to accept or reject Global's offer was next Monday, and Dustin wasn't any closer to figuring out what he should do than he'd been three weeks ago. He shot off another e-mail to Stefan, asking him if he could come to his office. A couple of minutes later there was a single knock on the door, followed by Stefan's head poking in.

"What's up?"

Dustin gestured for him to come inside. He waited for Stefan to take a seat before he gave him an abbreviated version of the back and forth he'd had with Global and several other companies that had inquired about buying him out over the past year. Dustin purposely left out the dollar amounts. The money didn't matter.

"Well, damn," Stefan said. "Your poker face has gotten better since those days on the carrier in the Persian Gulf. I had no idea you were even contemplating selling. You hid it well."

"I hid it for too long," Dustin said. "Now I'm up against the clock and have no idea what I'm going to do."

"Do you *want* to sell?"

"I want to fly," Dustin said. "I'm tired of being stuck behind this desk all the time."

"Damn, man. Do you have cotton between your ears?" Stefan sounded disgusted.

"What's that supposed to mean?"

"That's what my dad used to ask me when he thought I wasn't paying attention. I usually wasn't, but that's beside the point." He pointed at Dustin. "You, on the other hand, need to pay attention when I tell you stuff."

"What stuff?"

"You don't have to do it all," Stefan said. "I understand that big Einstein brain of yours thinks that it can do everything, but that's bull. You need to bring in a corporate organizer to help restructure the company. They come in, figure out what different departments you need, and help you find the right people to bring in."

"How do you know all of this?"

"I've been looking into it since we talked the other day."

"Well, why didn't you say anything to me about it?"

Stefan shrugged. "You never asked."

Dustin ran a hand down his face. "You can be a real asshole sometimes, you know that? I was on the verge of selling my company. Do you know how miserable I would have been if I'd given this all up for that eighty million dollars?"

"Eighty million dollars?" Stefan sprung up from his chair. "You didn't say they were offering *that* much."

"It's not about the money," Dustin said, rising from his chair and walking around his desk.

"The hell it's not," Stefan said. "Sell it. Wait, no, bring me in as a partner and *then* sell it."

"Come on," Dustin said, putting his arm

around his friend's shoulders. "I think I'll order some pizzas for the crew. They don't have to know what I originally called them into the conference room for, do they?"

His steps felt lighter now that he'd tackled this problem with Global that had been weighing so heavily on him. Now, he just had to solve the problem weighing on his heart.

Chapter Eight

Stef handed her keys to the valet before entering the wrought iron gate he held open for her.

"Follow the path to the rear gardens, ma'am," he said, pointing to the lighted walkway that curved around the left side of the house.

She took a minute to collect herself, taking several deep breaths.

You can do this.

Yes, she'd made a mistake, and over the past twenty-four hours she'd convinced herself that she was a big enough person to own up to it. She'd come to know Dustin well enough over these few short weeks to know that he would forgive her for her stubbornness, but that didn't make having to apologize and admit just how wrong she was any easier.

"But you're going to do it," Stef muttered to herself.

He deserved her apology. He deserved to know just how much he'd come to mean to her — the sheer bliss he'd brought into her life these past few weeks. He deserved to hear her say that she wanted what they'd started in Turks and Caicos to continue.

Following the path the valet had directed her to take, Stef came upon the second gate, the one that led to the side of the backyard where the hedge garden was located.

She was only forty minutes late, but the party was already in full swing.

A deejay played old-school hip hop and R&B—Stefan and Callie's music of choice—from a table tucked along the backend of the gardens. There was a full bar near the pool house, along with several servers who walked around with trays of hors d'oeuvres courtesy of Kiera Coleman's catering company.

She spotted the dessert buffet Dustin had told her about when she'd come over on Thursday. The desserts looked more like works of art than anything that was edible. They all were decorated in the wedding colors of coral and sage, which Dustin had purposely used as the party's color scheme.

Her gaze traveled over the crowd, searching for the one person she most wanted to see. Their eyes connected and a bolt of electricity shot through Stefanie's bloodstream.

Dustin stood at the other end of the pool, in a group with three other men. His legs were braced slightly apart, with one hand slung casually in his pocket while the other nursed a glass of amber liquid. From the outside, he was the picture of relaxed indifference. Except for his eyes. They bore into hers, penetrating. Intense.

Channeling the resolve that she'd built up over the hour-long drive from Maplesville, Stefanie started toward him.

A second later, she heard, "Hey, Stef! Over here."

She looked to the right and saw Callie waving her over to join a group from the wedding—Kiera and Jada, with their respective boyfriends, Trey Watson and Mason Coleman. Before she could decide which direction to take, Stefan intercepted her.

"Hey, you. It's about time you got here." Her twin greeted her with a kiss on the cheek.

Stef looked over his shoulder and saw Callie vigorously shaking her head. Good. She hadn't missed the big reveal. "How's my nephew?" Stefan asked. "I meant to stop by the house to see him yesterday, but got caught up at work."

"He wouldn't have been there. He's got too many social commitments."

Her brother's brow creased in confusion.

Stef waved her hand. "Don't ask. Just know that he is doing fine. Shelia and Robert spoiled him silly."

"As grandparents should."

She glanced toward where she'd spotted Dustin, but he was no longer there.

"Here, let me introduce you around," Stefan said, wrapping an arm around her and guiding her to a cluster of men and women. All were

Hawk Offshore Transportation employees. All were also ex-military personnel, and all had great things to say about her brother.

"I paid them to say this stuff," Stefan joked.

Once she was finally able to politely break away, Stef sought Dustin again, but as soon as she headed in his direction, he turned the other way. Over the next hour, she made eye contact with him several times, but whenever she tried to move toward him, he managed to find someplace else to be.

Pain sliced through her at the realization that he was actively avoiding her. She deserved it after the way she'd repeatedly rejected him. She realized how arrogant it was of her to think that all she needed to do was apologize to Dustin to make everything right again — as if her admitting that she was wrong was all it would take.

Jada caught her by the hand. "Callie's about to give Stefan his gift," she whispered, dragging her over to join Kiera.

At the table reserved for wedding gifts. Callie reached underneath the sage green table skirt and pulled out a gift bag. The pastel colors — pink, blue, and yellow — were a big clue as to the surprise, not that Stef's oblivious brother noticed. When Callie handed him the book, he just kissed her cheek and set it on the table.

Callie picked the book up and shoved it back

at him. Confusion clouded Stefan's face as he thumbed through the pages. Stef could tell he had no idea why Callie wanted him to look at a bunch of old pictures in the middle of a party.

As he neared the rear pages, his movements slowed. He got to the final page and his jaw dropped. When he looked at Callie, she nodded as tears streamed down her face.

Stef had to wipe her own cheeks, while Kiera and Jada sniffled through their teary-eyed smiles.

In a voice loud enough for everyone in New Orleans to hear, Stefan yelled, "We're having a baby!" He picked Callie up and twirled her around in his arms.

The crowd erupted in excited cheers. A line quickly formed with guests eager to congratulate the expectant parents.

Stef managed to slip in and give her brother and sister-in-law hugs before disengaging from the enthusiastic fray surrounding them. Once again, she sought out Dustin. When she spotted him going inside through the kitchen door, she took off after him.

She found him standing at the large granite island. He was tipping a bottle of champagne over flutes on a silver serving tray, filling them halfway. A woman in black pants and a tuxedo shirt with the *Catering by Kiera* logo embroidered over the left breast stood to his right, arranging more glasses on another tray. A second server entered the kitchen carrying an empty tray over one shoulder. She quickly started to fill it with Kiera's in-demand crab tarts.

Stef's steps slowed as she neared the island. She stopped directly across from Dustin. Several intense moments ticked by while she waited for the servers to leave. As he set the bottle of champagne down, for a second, she thought he was going to leave too.

She refused to let him slip away again. "Are you purposely avoiding me?" she asked, going straight to the heart of the matter.

"I'm hosting a party," Dustin returned.

"So, you're the type of host who deliberately avoids speaking to his guests?"

"What do you want from me, Stefanie? I'm trying to respect your wishes."

"I never wanted you to walk the other way when you see me," she managed to say past the regret tightening her throat.

"Shit," Dustin whispered. He came around the kitchen island and caught Stef by the wrist. He drew her into the spacious dining room adjacent to the kitchen. The moment he shut the door behind them, he dropped her hand and started to pace back and forth in the space between the ten-person table and the marble fireplace.

"You're the one who said it had to end," Dustin said. He stopped in front of her and held up both hands. "I'm only doing what you asked."

"I said that we couldn't see each other anymore, not that you should pretend that you don't see me at all. You can at least talk to me."

"No, I can't." He shook his head. "I can't talk to you, because seeing you here tonight and knowing that I can no longer be with you is killing me. Although, it's not as if avoiding you has dulled the pain all that much either."

The hurt in his voice squeezed at her chest. "Dustin, I never meant to hurt you," she said. "You have no idea how sorry I am."

"Yeah, well, you're not the only one." He shook his head. "I keep telling myself that it would have been better if I'd walked right past you at that bar on Grand Turk, but that's a damn lie. If I had to go back and do things differently, I wouldn't change a single thing, not if it means giving up the time we shared these past two weeks.

"But do me a favor, Stefanie. Don't make it any harder than it has to be. I'm avoiding you tonight because it's easier that way."

He turned and walked over to the window that faced the gardens. His back was rigid, everything about him screaming *do not approach*.

She ignored the silent warning, walking over to him and stopping just a few feet away. After several tries, Stef finally said, "What if those are no longer my wishes?"

His posture stiffened even more, his head

jerking up. Slowly, he turned to face her. A mask of doubt clouded his face, but there was a glimmer of hope reflected in his intense stare.

His words, when he spoke them, were so soft she could barely hear them. "What are you saying?"

Ribbons of uncertainty and apprehension knotted in her belly. The probability of him dismissing her from his life was higher than she cared to contemplate.

But of all the risks she'd ever taken in life, this one had the greatest reward.

"I'm saying I was wrong not to give us a chance," she stated. "I'm saying that I was wrong not to trust my own strength not to turn back into that girl I was all those years ago." She brought her eyes to his and held his stare, swiping at the insolent tear that escaped despite her best effort to hold it back.

"And I'm sorry for not trusting in what we had," she said.

"Stefanie—"

She put her hand up, staving off his reply. "I was afraid that being with you would turn me back into that girl I've worked so hard to leave behind, but then I remembered that she wasn't all bad. There was good in her, and you brought out the very best parts. You reminded me that it's okay to enjoy life, and then you showed me how to do it."

Stef swallowed back the emotion that

climbed up from her throat. "But I've come to realize that I won't enjoy a life that doesn't have you in it. I want to give us a chance, Dustin. Are you willing to take that chance with me?"

His chest expanded with the deep breath he inhaled.

"I don't know if I can," he said.

Stef blinked several times, momentarily caught off-guard by his response.

Expected him to just fall over with gratitude?

Yes, she had. She hadn't realized just how overconfident she was until her arrogance had come back to bite her in the ass for the second time today.

Doing her best to disguise the hurt in her voice, Stef nodded and said, "I understand."

She turned to leave, but Dustin caught her by the arm and pulled her against his chest.

"Get over here." He cradled her face in his hands. "I was going to make you sweat for a bit, but I want to kiss you too damn much."

He crushed his lips to hers in a kiss that had her simultaneously sighing in relief and begging for more.

"That probably wasn't the best time to joke around, was it?" Dustin whispered against her lips.

"No," she said. "But I don't care. As long as you promise it won't be the last."

Seconds drifted into minutes as they stood there wrapped in each other's embrace. Stef had no idea how much time had passed when she heard her brother's voice calling out from the kitchen.

"In there?" The door to the dining room opened. "Hey, where—Aw, shit." Stefan put his hands up. "I don't want to know what's happening. I just want to know if you have one of those big nets for fishing stuff out of the pool. Someone's shoe ended up in there."

"There's a closet on the left side of the pool house," Dustin said.

"Okay, thanks." Stefan looked between the two of them and shook his head. He mumbled something that sounded like, "I should kick your ass," before he backed out of the dining room and closed the door behind him.

"I'm not worried about him," Dustin said. "He's all talk." He dropped his hands to her waist, his fingers meeting at the small of her back.

"I guess you should get back out there," Stef said. "You *do* have a party to host."

"They're grown. They can fend for themselves."

He leaned forward and captured her lips in a kiss that made her forget about the backyard full of party guests just steps away. It made her forget about everything. Everything but him.

Epilogue

Stef pounded her fist on the tabletop, trying her hardest to fight the disgust crawling over her skin. She rocked back and forth, her eyes closed tight. She slowly sucked in a deep breath, and then blew it out on an equally deep exhale.

"Come on, Mom," Jacob whined.

"Yeah, come on," Dustin said. "This isn't some yoga routine. Get to it."

Stef cocked one eye open and speared them both with a death glare. "Can you two give me just one minute?"

"We've been sitting here for twenty," Dustin said. "Stop stalling."

She held her hands up. "Look, I don't have to do this if I don't want to. Neither of you can make me."

"But you said you would," Jacob pointed out as he lifted the tortilla chip from the paper plate and carried it over to her.

"That's right," Dustin said. A grin slid across his face. "Now, open wide."

You are going to pay for this, she mouthed.

Stef tried to avert her eyes, but she wasn't quick enough. She caught sight of the fried cricket sitting on top of the chip and nearly lost her breakfast.

"Wouldn't the next step in this bug therapy thing be touching it?" she asked Dustin. "How did we jump all the way to eating already?"

"Would you please hurry this up?" Dustin said, heavy on the exaggerated frustration. "Stefan and I are interviewing candidates for the HR department head position in less than an hour. Now that he's taking over some of the management duties, your brother has turned into the biggest hard a—" He glanced at Jacob. "Hard nose I know. Will you eat the bug already so I can head back to work?"

"Stop rushing me," Stef said. "Didn't you come here by helicopter? You can get back to work in five minutes."

Jacob started to chant, "Eat-the-bug. Eat-the-bug."

Dustin joined in, along with the kids at the table next to theirs. If she didn't get this over with soon everyone in the Insectarium would be here, pressuring her to snack on this cricket.

Dustin held up a hand, halting the chant. "Hold on, fellas. I know how to get her to eat it."

He'd better not…

Dustin took the chip from Jacob's hand and held it in front of her. With a wicked grin lifting up the corner of his mouth, he said, "I dare you."

He did. Oh, he was so going to pay for this.

With an arrogant arch to her brow, Stefanie snatched the chip and, just before popping it in her mouth, said, "You're on."

Thank you so much for purchasing and reading *I Dare You*.

Read the entire Moments in Maplesville series:
A Perfect Holiday Fling (Callie & Stefan)
A Little Bit Naughty (Jada & Mason)
Just a Little Taste (Kiera and Trey)

The Holmes Brother Series:
Set in New Orleans, the Holmes Brothers series follows the lives of Elijah, Tobias, and Alexander Holmes as they find love in one of the world's most romantic cities.

Read *Deliver Me, Release Me*, and *Rescue Me*, available both individually and in a special bundle edition!
Get all three books in the Holmes Brothers series for one low price!

In Her Wildest Dreams
Event planner Erica Cole recruits her best friend to help her plan the ultimate Valentine's Day fantasy, but chocolatier Gavin Foster is determined to show her that they should be

more than just friends.

The Rebound Guy

Relationship advisor Dexter Bryant is trying to shake his stud-for-hire image, but when Asia Carpenter makes him an offer he can't refuse, Dex will have to play the role of professional rebound guy one last time.

Romances from Harlequin Kimani!

The New York Sabers

*Don't miss my sizzling **New York Sabers** football series! Check my website for details!*

Bayou Dreams

Check out my brand new series set in the small, fictional town of Gauthier, Louisiana!

About the Author:

A native of south Louisiana, *USA Today* Bestselling author Farrah Rochon officially began her writing career while waiting in between classes in the student lounge at Xavier University of Louisiana. After earning her Bachelors of Science degree and a Masters of Arts from Southeastern Louisiana University, Farrah decided to pursue her lifelong dream of becoming a published novelist. She was named *Shades of Romance Magazine*'s Best New Author of 2007. Her debut novel garnered rave reviews, earning Farrah several SORMAG Readers' Choice Awards. *I'll Catch You*, the second book in her New York Sabers series for Harlequin Kimani, was a 2012 RITA[R] Award finalist.

When she is not writing in her favorite coffee shop, Farrah spends most of her time reading her favorite romance novels or seeing as many Broadway shows as possible. An admitted sports fanatic, Farrah feeds her addiction to football by watching New Orleans Saints games on Sunday afternoons.

71124024R00109

Made in the USA
Middletown, DE
20 April 2018

Holy Cross and ikons; and they observed the laws of Moses and kept Saturday instead of Sunday as a day of rest. Some of the heretical priests were brought by Ivan III from Novgorod to Moscow and installed in the court cathedrals of that city where they worked quietly and made many converts, even in high places. The heresy spread so fast that Archbishop Gennadius of Novgorod made complaints to Moscow, but the case was not pushed with vigor. In order to arouse the Moscow authorities Gennadius secured the coöperation of the influential Joseph Volotski. Joseph denounced the heresy vigorously and demanded the death penalty for the heretics. In this, again, he was opposed by the Trans-Volga monks, who wrote against such cruelty in the name of Christ. In this case, as in the dispute over the monastic lands, the views of Joseph won. At the general church council of 1504 the heretics were condemned to death, and many of them were burned at the stake.

Such were the principal subjects dealt with in the literature of Moscow at the close of the fifteenth and beginning of the sixteenth centuries. The Josephites supported the idea of autocracy and the established religious order, and were, in turn, supported by the grand princes.